I0757740

Something Gained

A Romantic Comedy

Chiquita Dennie

Copyright © 2021 by Chiquita Dennie

All rights reserved.

No part of this book may be reproduced in any form or by any electronic or mechanical means, including information storage and retrieval systems, without written permission from the author, except for the use of brief quotations in a book review.

This is a work of fiction. Names, characters, places, and incidents are either the product of the author's imagination or are used fictitiously, and any resemblance to actual persons, living or dead, business establishments, events or locales is entirely coincidental.

For questions and comments about this book, please contact info@ 304publishing.com at www.chiquitadennie.com

 Created with Vellum

Disclaimer

This work of fiction contains strong language and explicit sexual content and is only intended for mature readers. This story may contain unconventional situations, language, and sexual encounters that may offend some readers. This book is for mature readers (18+).

Latest Releases from Chiquita Dennie

Latest Releases from Chiquita Dennie

The Early Years-A Prequel Short Story

Antonio and Sabrina: Struck in Love 1, 2, 3, 4, 5

Heart of Stone, Book 1 (Emery & Jackson)

Heart Of Stone Book 1.5 Emery &Jackson A Valentine's Day Short

Janice and Carlo: Captivated By His Love

Heart of Stone, Book 2 (Jordan and Damon)

Temptation

Heart of Stone, Book 3 (Angela and Brent)

Cocky Catcher

Bossy Billionaire

Bottoms Up Heart of Stone, Book 3.5 (Jessica and Joseph Short

Love Shorts: A Collection of Short Stories

Joaquin Fuertes (The Fuertes Cartel Book 1)

Exposed (Salvation Society Novel)

Joaquin Fuertes (The Fuertes Cartel Book 2)

Refuel (A Driven World Novel)

Pressure (A Driven World Novel)
Until Serena (HEA World Novel)
Antonio and Sabrina: Struck in Love 5
Heart of Stone, Book 4 (Jessica and Joseph)
She's All I Need
Red Light District (A Fantasy Romance)
Something Gained (A Romantic Comedy)
Upcoming Releases (2022/2023):
Something Gained (A Romantic Comedy Book 1)
Aydin-TN Security Book 1
Dare To Love
The Carrington Cartel Book 1
Something Earned (A Romantic Comedy Book 2)
The Carrington Cartel Book 2

Introduction

Are you signed up for my newsletter?

Join today and find out all the latest in new releases, contests, giveaways, sneak peeks, and more.
www.chiquitadennie.com

Synopsis

Ava ~

With \$500,000 on the line, I refuse to lose the *America's Next Top Chemist* competition. It's mine for the taking. I put in all the work. I am at the top of my game. I can do this... or so I thought until my leading competitor—my smart, sexy, and ultra-cocky long-time rival, Blaze, walks in the door and threatens my chances.

Blaze ~

The grand prize is mine. I didn't work this hard for this long to walk away empty-handed. I'm the top chemist in California. How can I lose? The answer is simple: Ava Johnston is my number one competitor—and the sexiest woman I've ever seen. I can't let her beauty distract me. That's the plan. The question is, can I stick to it?

Chapter One

Ava

It was supposed to be my best day ever. I was about to compete in the highest-rated show on television, *America's Next Top Chemist*. As a biochemist, it was an honor to be able to show the world that science can be both deep and engaging. After celebrating my acceptance the night before with my best friend, Trisha, it had already turned into a spooky day since I woke up late.

Due to an allergic reaction in the restaurant, I developed hives on my arms, probably triggered by food that had peanut oil in it.

"Nothing can be simple." I looked in the mirror, and the swelling was still noticeable.

When I cleaned up the pollen from my furniture, I ended up with red, swollen eyes. Trisha offered to take me to the hospital if I needed, but I knew I'd be okay as long as she could help me administer my EpiPen. The early morning alarm went off, and I went into a panic, thinking I was running behind. I jumped out of bed, remembering I'd scheduled a taxi service. I hit the railing between the bedpost and nightstand while running out of bed and stubbed my toe.

"Ugrhhh!" I hopped around, rubbing the sting away.

The mistake I made was thinking it would be easy to get to my flight on time after I showered and got dressed. There were long lines, terrible food, and a crying baby next to me. Once I got to Miami six hours later, my flight had lost my luggage, and I found myself getting out of the car service with only my carry-on. As I pulled my skirt down, I closed the door of the Uber and held my phone between my shoulder and ear.

"Hey, get out of the way!" a young kid on a skateboard shouted, almost hitting me.

"This is the sidewalk!" I fussed.

The wind wasn't cooperating today. The weather app I'd checked before arriving here said around ninety degrees. Therefore, I'd put on a strapless, flowery dress with wedge heels.

"Did you make it safe?" Trisha, pulled me away from distraction of the kid. She and I had known each other since college five years ago. She was a veterinarian and the same age as me: twenty-six. She had medium length hair and brown skin and was a little shorter than my five-seven.

I can say I wouldn't have gotten through college without her carefree spirit.

I stepped through the crowd, looked up at the Miami Cascade Hotel, and sighed in relaxation after the debacle of my day.

"Finally made it to the hotel. Today has been the craziest situation I've ever dealt with," I groaned as I pushed forward into the revolving door, gripping my bag close to me. Just as I pushed, an older guy shifted forward, and my skirt got caught in between the doors.

"Shit!"

"Hurry up!" he shouted.

"You see me holding a bag, sir," I growled and yanked on my skirt.

"What happened to you, Ava?"

"Let me call you back, Trisha."

"No, keep me on the phone."

"Can you look away, please?" I asked as the doorman came over to try and help me.

"I've seen it all," he responded, and my mouth opened, then shut, not ready to blow my top. I had a great opportunity to make a name for myself and to end up online or worse, arrested for arguing with an old guy with a potbelly and a bad toupee.

"Sir, back up a few steps," the doorman told him, and he rolled his eyes, finally motioning for the person behind him to go backwards. People have no manners anymore, and it pisses me off how society is just rude no matter what issue arises. Finally, I got loose and walked over to stand in line. There were about four people in front of me.

"You okay?"

"Yes. My skirt got caught in the door."

"Maybe I should have come with you."

"No, I need to do this alone."

I hadn't told Trisha the secret of why I wanted to win this money, and it wasn't just for CrimsonBio. The funds would be split between CrimsonBio and the local community center that helped inspire my love for science through middle school and high school.

"I woke up late and hit my toe, plus the airline lost most of my clothes. I'm so glad today is almost over. I just need to check in, then I can relax and eat before really getting started with anything."

"Damn, do you need anything?"

"No, I should be fine. I have my carry-on and purse. I can go shopping later today or tomorrow. The entire competition is five days, and they have us here for seven with a bonus day to hang out," I replied.

I glanced around the hotel. I could see it was fancy, and I was really surprised. They had everything here. It had a Mediterranean feel, complete with an open fountain and a pond, as well as high ceilings with crystal chandeliers. I looked at the rooms they had us in, and they weren't cheap either. I was kind of looking forward to spending the next week or so in a place that was far more luxurious than anyplace I'd ever been in before.

"What time is Melody getting there?" Trisha asked.

Melody Robinson was my other best friend and my boss at CrimsonBio. Working alongside her had been a blessing for me. She understood my quirky personality, that I was introverted and still appreciated me for who I was. I worked as the lead director of CrimsonBio, and if we won the grand prize of $500,000, we could upgrade some of our equipment, hire more staff, and work on getting more media attention for our female-owned business. I lifted my watch, checking the time.

"She should get here in two or three days. I should be fine by myself. She's mostly here for moral support." I moved up to the counter, pulled out my ID, and passed it to the attendant.

"Welcome to Miami Cascade Hotel."

"Thank you. I should have a room under the competition show," I said.

She smiled and typed in my information.

"Ma'am, it looks like your reservation isn't here and the

hotel is booked up for the week," she replied, passing back my ID.

"I'm sorry, you must have typed in the wrong name." I leaned over the counter, and she typed in my name again. I could hear Trisha on the other end of the phone asking what the problem was. The hotel clerk turned her screen around toward me only for me to see that my name wasn't on the registry.

"Your name's not on the list. Sorry."

"That's not possible. I have a confirmation and everything. Please check again or call your manager," I fussed, making sure to not drop my carry-on.

"Ma'am, we have a lengthy line behind you. Can you take a seat? I will have someone come out to speak with you," the hotel clerk stated.

I turned, looking over my shoulder, and the last person I expected to see was behind me. *The Blaze Newton*, another biologist, the owner of his own firm, and a chemist by trade. Around the industry, he was known as the flirt. The number of women that talked about sleeping with him was insane. Also, he was cocky, stubborn, and believed he was God's gift to women. I grunted, angling my weight from one foot to the other.

"Trisha, let me call you back." I hung up, not waiting for her to reply.

"Ava, I didn't know that was you." Blaze closed his own phone.

"Hey," I answered dryly.

"Someone's grumpy," he responded, chuckling.

I stepped out of line and walked over to the waiting area. My feet were killing me, and all I wanted to do was eat and shower. I pulled my shades down to look in the mirror on the wall. My eyes were looking better. Once the stress of the day was over, I could relax and take more medicine.

Hearing a throat clear, I looked up and saw Blaze hovering over me.

"What's with the long face?" he asked.

"Blaze, leave me alone," I groaned.

"Ava, come on, you look like shit, baby."

"Whatever!" I snapped, rolling my eyes and pulling my purse into my lap.

That only gave him what he wanted, and he burst out in laughter.

"Seriously, what's the problem?"

"You're the competition. I can't talk to you now," I told him.

"I promise I won't steal any ideas, I kind of overheard you talking with the hotel manager about your room." He pointed over to the counter.

I nodded in answer.

"Somehow my reservation got lost or given away. Plus, the airline lost my luggage, and I'm dealing with swollen eyes from a terrible allergy attack. That about sums up my life at the moment."

"Well, I can't help with the swollen eyes or anything. But you can come stay with me in my room until they fix everything," Blaze stated.

"No, I can't do that," I said, shaking my head.

"I know my reputation as a ladies' man is running around the circuit, but I'm not a bad guy. Nothing will happen, and you need to get a hot bath and food in your stomach." He stood up and extended a hand for me.

"I don't want to put you out." Deep down, I didn't want to have a sex dream about him and accidentally call out his name again. *Don't judge me*. The man was cute with dimples on both sides of his face and a long beard that I'd love to run my fingers through. He was tall, at six-two, and slim but muscular, without overdoing it like some guys. The worst part was I knew he was a womanizer and never would commit.

"I upgraded to a suite when I found out I got accepted. Don't worry about the space. Besides, you can probably learn a few things from me that can help you on the show," he joked, and I slapped his hand away.

"I really can't stand you," I seethed before I stood up to follow him to the elevator. He grabbed my bag, and we walked almost in sync to the bank of elevators.

Stepping onto the elevator, he pushed the button 'S' for suites, and I stood back against the wall, closing my eyes as the elevator doors closed.

"You look cute," I heard him say.

"I feel like shit."

"Naw, you're fine, besides the swollen eyes and bandage on your big toe. I'd go out with you," Blaze teased, and the elevator door chimed, letting us know we had arrived at our floor. He motioned for me to step off first and reached for my bag, but I waved him off.

"I can carry it myself."

"Don't insult me." He took the bag out of my hands.

"I won't be here long. As soon as I get things fixed at the front desk," I explained, knowing he would probably throw this back in my face. The key light turned green.

"You can have the bed."

"This feels weird," I stated.

"What do you mean?" he questioned, pushing the door open to let me walk in first. I glanced around the suite in awe. The place was gorgeous and spacious, big enough for at least three or four people. Now I was curious why he needed a suite when it was only him taking part in the competition.

"Why are you being nice to me? Normally we don't talk unless it's at a conference. Most of the time you look over me toward the girls that fall over you and praise your every move." I took my bag back and set it near the couch.

"Ava, I've always noticed you. You're just too caught up in what other people think and say." Blaze dropped his luggage on the floor and headed to the liquor bar.

"Yeah, right. Anyway, what are you planning for the show?" I probed as I took the water bottle he passed me from the fridge.

"I'm not telling you my secrets. Besides, I'm saving all the good stuff for presentation day." Blaze sat down on the couch, picked up the remote, and kicked off his shoes.

"Mmmmmm...Melody is coming to help me, and I'm a huge fan of the show, having watched it over the past few years. After three times of applying, I finally got picked to be included."

I went to the chair near the end of the table and took a seat, pulled my cell out, and sent a text to Trisha.

Me: They messed up my room.
Trisha: What! Where are you?
Me: You wouldn't believe it.
Trisha: Tell me?
Me: Blaze offered to let me stay in his room.
Trisha: How do we feel about that?

I peered over at him as he was glued to the football game on TV.

Me: I'm annoyed they lost my room.
Trisha: We'll make the most of it.
Me: What do you mean?
Trisha: See what Blaze is working with.

"I think not," I blurted out.

"Think not what?"

"Huh? Nothing," I replied.

"Tell your girlfriends I don't bite." He chuckled and stood up, walking back to the kitchen of the suite.

Me: I can't stay here long.

Trisha: Did you pack up Peter?

I chuckled and covered my mouth, thinking about my vibrator we'd named Peter—well, really *Pussy Popping Peter*.

Me: Let me get off this phone.

Trisha: You've always wanted to have a threesome :)

I snorted at her response.

Me: Goodbye Trisha.

"Can I use your bathroom?" I closed out of the text message thread and went to grab my things so I could freshen up and find a shop to grab a few items to hold me over.

"Fifty dollars."

"Excuse me?" My eyes turned into slits.

"I have a reputation to keep up."

"Well, your reputation—"

He held his hand up to interrupt and laughed.

"I'm joking. You can use the restroom."

Blaze is my enemy, Blaze is my enemy, I repeated over and over in my mind to remember this was a competition and not to mess around with him.

"Of course he has a nice ass," I muttered low when he bent over to grab something out of his bag.

"What was that?" he called out as I strolled by him.

I entered the bathroom and shut the door.

"Nothing!"

* * *

I stared back at my image, wanting to scream at how the day had completely drained me of any energy. I smelled under my arms and screwed up my face.

"Shower time."

I'd wash my hair tomorrow, but right now I needed to get cleaned up and find a shop to buy some clothes. I placed my carry-on bag on the counter, noticing that my favorite bodywash was in my lost luggage. I only used specific body-washes after realizing that some of the chemicals in soaps broke me out. I was committed to using organic or vegan soap on my light brown skin and especially on my curly hair. I pulled out my hair clip, then removed my skirt, shirt, and underwear and tossed them in the side pocket of my bag. Sauntering to the shower, I turned it to the hottest temperature and shifted to remove a towel from the cabinet over the toilet. I slid the door back and hopped in the shower.

"I needed this." I picked up the hotel bodywash and poured a nice amount in a towel and washed my back and arms. Bobbing to the music in my head, I hovered over and wiped up and down my left leg when the water from the shower head blasted me in the face with a full-on stream.

"Awhhh!"

I moved forward to turn it off, slipped, and landed on my back.

"Oh shit!"

The door burst open, and I was even more embarrassed to have been beaten up by a damn showerhead.

"What the fuck!" Blaze blurted out, sliding the shower door open and turning the water off.

"I'm fine!" I tried to turn and cover myself but felt a twinge in my back.

"Here, take this." Blaze handed me a towel.

"Thanks." I bit on my bottom lip. Of course to top off not having my room ready this happens. I shook my head in annoyance.

"Do you need help standing?"

"No."

"You sure?"

He was taking pleasure in my misery.

"Turn around, and I'll just use your body to stand up."

"Just like a woman to use me for my body," he cackled.

"Am I being punked?" I looked around the bathroom for a camera.

"What?"

"Nothing." Grumbling, I pushed myself off the floor, wrapped the towel tighter around my body, and slowly grabbed on to his leg and hand to pull myself up.

Chapter Two

Blaze

Ava Johnston was a pain in the ass. I knew once I got accepted, she would probably be included this season. She was friends with Melody and her husband, who were also close friends of mine, and ever since Ava found out I was honest when dealing with women and never catered to other people's feelings, she wrote me off as a playboy, all about pussy and nothing else. The truth was that I just had standards. Overall, I wasn't looking to get tied down to any woman, especially when my company was slowly gaining traction in a hugely competitive market. The data we'd collected from years of testing and research would make Newton Industries much more attractive for major funding and donations as a private company. I would never apologize for my success, and if a woman couldn't understand the time and sacrifice it took to be one of the few African American biochemist firms in the country, then she would definitely not be someone I could count on in the awful times.

Once I helped her in the bathroom, I left her alone to

get dressed and went back to the living room to grab a few things I needed to shower and change into. Plus, I was hungry and wanted to order some food. Underneath that hard exterior was a beautiful woman with a nice figure I'd had many dreams and fantasies about. She was just shy of five-six or seven, with a curvy, slim figure.

"Are you hungry?" I grabbed the menu off the table, flipping through the dinner and lunch section. She had a slight limp as she walked over to the couch while wearing the same clothes she had worn before. Her high hair allowed me to see her dark brown eyes, soft pillowy lips, and pointy nose more prominently.

"I could go for some food, but I need to get to a store."

"Most stores around here can deliver."

"No, I like to go in and try the clothes on."

"Suit yourself, but we have orientation soon." I checked the time on my watch.

"Damn it! I forgot about that."

"Yeah, it's mostly to sign in and meet the other contestants."

As her lips pursed, she kicked her right foot against the ground while crossing her arms.

"Shit!" she groaned and bent down to rub what I assumed was the sore leg from the shower.

"Go right ahead and take the bed. I'll tell them you weren't feeling good."

"You'd like that." She grabbed the menu from me and sat down on the couch.

"I'm not the enemy."

"I can take the couch."

I raised my hand to interrupt her reply.

"What kind of man would I be if I allowed you to sleep

on the couch? I'm not an awful guy, Ava, no matter what you've heard." I reached for her sore leg and placed it in my lap. Ava was funny, but stubborn. We clashed often at conferences on certain ways to get the solution to a science problem. I wasn't expecting to offer up my room to her, but I'd felt bad when I saw how she looked after the hotel clerk told her about the mix-up with her room.

"What are you doing?" She tried to remove her leg.

"Relax. I've been known to give a great massage."

"That leads to my clothes being off and you seducing me."

"Are you serious?" I wrinkled my nose.

"I heard you've slept with half the women in the industry." She lay back on the couch and closed her eyes, then yawned.

Chuckling at her annoyance, I finished her massage, then stood up and stretched.

"Don't believe everything you hear, Ava. How about you order enough food for us both? I need to make a call really quickly." I took my phone from my pocket, opened the balcony door, and walked out.

I called Diego's number. I stared back at Ava as I eagerly awaited an answer.

"Hello," I said once he picked up.

"You made it to Miami?" he asked.

"I did, and you wouldn't believe who I ran into," I responded, glancing over my shoulder. The living room was clear, so I peeked inside and noticed that Ava had left the bedroom door open. I couldn't turn away when I saw her bent over, smoothing lotion on both of her legs, not wearing any underwear.

"Who is it?" Diego asked, bringing me back to my senses.

"Uhhhhmmm...Ava." I cleared my throat.

"Ava? Melody's best friend, Ava Johnston?"

"Yep. I was in line behind her, and her hotel room somehow got overbooked or mixed up, and she didn't have anywhere to stay. I offered my suite."

"Ohhh, shit," he said laughing.

"What's funny?"

"Leave her alone, Blaze. I know you, and as your best friend I'm telling you, don't break that girl's heart."

"I have no intention of breaking anyone's heart, because I'm only here to win the grand prize money of five hundred thousand," I insisted.

"You say that now."

"You act like I can't control myself."

"Blaze, come on. Before I got married I was your right-hand man on the dating scene. I know what you're capable of and the type of women you sleep with. Ava's a good girl."

As I pondered Ava in that light, I heard the doorbell ring. I walked back inside, hearing loud music coming from the bedroom. I let room service inside and pulled out my wallet to pay.

"Keep the change," I said, and he nodded.

"Thank you, sir."

I lifted the top off the tray and saw burgers, fries, chocolate cake, and tacos.

"Who was that?" Diego questioned.

"Room service. Let me go tell Ava it's here." I walked over to the bedroom, knocked, and got no answer. I figured she was in the bathroom, so I called from the door.

"Hold on, Diego."

"Yeah."

I moved the phone away from my ear.

"Food is here!"

"All right," she replied, and a few seconds later, the door opened, and we stood staring at each other.

"What? Do I have something on my face?"

"No, sorry."

"Blaze!"

"Someone's calling your name." She pointed at the phone.

"Shit! Sorry, Diego."

"Man, what are you doing?" he fussed. I moved back, letting Ava walk over to the tray of food. She lifted the top and clapped her hands in excitement.

"This looks good." She picked up a french fry and popped it in her mouth.

"What was that? Is she all right?" Diego asked.

"Yeah, the food just got here," I said, biting my bottom lip.

Ava was sexy with her curvy hips and plump ass. I loved a woman that was confident in her body and wasn't afraid to eat in front of me. She bit into the burger and held it up with a Thumbs-up at me. I've never been shy when it comes to my preferences of the type of women I date.

"Melody will kill you, man," Diego taunted.

I angled to the tray and grabbed my plate, sitting next to her on the couch. I wasn't scared of Melody and didn't have anything to worry about when it came to me and Ava in the dating sense. We weren't each other's type, and dating wasn't on my agenda while I ran my business and tried to win this money.

"Diego, I'll call you back." I didn't wait for him to answer.

"This might be the best burger I've ever eaten."

"It's not bad. So tell me why you're competing." I opened a water bottle and took a gulp.

"Same reason as you. Money." She sat up on the couch with her legs crossed underneath her.

"You might as well step aside, because I have it on lock."

As I frowned at her overblown expression, she cackled.

"You can calm down with your overdramatic laughter."

That only made her go full-blown belly-holding laughter. I dropped my burger on my plate and rose off the couch, and she reached for my arm to stop me.

"Wait! I'm sorry. Sit back down."

"I need to go check in downstairs."

"Ah, poor baby got his feelings hurt."

"Whatever, Ava. At least I have clothes and a room."

She stopped laughing at that comment and flipped me off. "Asshole."

I put the plate in the fridge for later when I got back.

"Anyway. Here's the other key to the room." I pulled the second keycard out of my pocket and handed it to her.

"Thanks. As soon as I clear up the room situation, I'll be out of your hair."

"You're good. May the best man win?" I extended my hand for a shake.

"May the best person win." She grasped my hand with a strong grip, and I smirked. She stood up with a twisted look on her face.

"I'm heading downstairs to check in."

"I'm coming too."

"Are you sure? I can tell them you'll check in later."

"No, I'm coming too. A lot is riding on this for me."

"Good luck getting past the check-in table."

"Why?" She looked down at herself.

"The attire is formal." I pointed at her outfit of choice and smiled.

"But I thought it was just—"

"You didn't look at the rules?"

I pulled my phone out of my pocket and went to the email with the details of the pre-check-in day. I passed my phone over to her.

"Crap!" she shouted, slapping the phone back in my hand, and began to pace back and forth. Anyone else in my shoes would have just walked out and forgotten about her, getting the upper hand with making an impression on the judges. But if I planned on winning, I wanted it to be fair and square.

"Look, I think there's a boutique in the hotel."

"Really?"

"Yeah, I don't know what time they close, but you can try and see if they have something."

She slipped her feet into the shoes she'd been wearing before and grabbed her purse.

"Wait!"

"What?"

"Aren't you going to apologize?"

"For what?"

"Uhm...for mischaracterizing me." I held the door open as we stepped out.

"I mean, it's still early," she snidely remarked.

I shut the door, walked to the elevator, and pushed the button.

"Hey!"

"Yeah?" I turned to look over my shoulder.

"I'm stuck in the door!"

"Good luck with that." I winked at her and stepped onto the elevator.

"Blaze! Blaze! You asshole."

* * *

"I hate shopping, and having to try on clothes exhausts me," Ava muttered.

She'd finally been able to unstick herself from the door and get down to the boutique to pick out a dress that was presentable for tonight. It wasn't overly dressy, but paired with a black jacket, it had an elegant look.

My phone rang in my pocket; I slipped it out and saw a call from Kenya. We'd ended our casual relationship seven months before because my work was too demanding. We'd never really been a couple, just two people having sex. I put my phone on silent. In her mind it was something more, but I never gave her any expectations of us being together.

"What?" I inquired, seeing Ava's raised eyebrow.

"You could have taken the call. Don't let me hinder you from getting laid," she stated, grabbing a bottle of water off the bar.

"Sex is the last thing on my mind. I'm here to win."

Her gaze took hold of mine, and I took advantage, sweeping down and back up to her pouty lips, which had a hint of red lipstick.

"I wouldn't get so confident, Blaze. Your charm won't win this time with the judges."

I chuckled at her frown.

"You keep bringing up my charm and me getting laid."

"Please don't stroke your own ego, sir."

"I have something else you can stroke."

A fake gag was her reply.

"Chemistry is the show's focus, not flirting. Thus, you should depart now." Ava raised her thumb at the exit door as if to say *Time to go.*

"Would you like to bet on that?" I asked, holding out my hand to seal the deal.

The coordinator called out names in alphabetical order and started to hand out passes for tomorrow. She shifted from one foot to the other, and I took a sip of my water and waited for her response.

Chapter Three

Ava

Despite my best efforts, my thoughts would not line up. My breathing changed every time his mouth moved or his eyes peered down at me. The majority of the time, when I find someone attractive, I can discern him, and I will pass him my number and we will meet for dinner. If I felt a connection with the guy, I would go out casually or for a hookup. I wasn't the type to shy away from my desires, but around Blaze, I felt distracted, my mouth dry. It was clear to me that he slept with many women, and probably not the same person more than once. Especially when they were competing against each other. Because of that, I wouldn't let his godlike looks distract me.

"What would I get if I won?"

He shrugged, then said, "I will help promote CrimsonBio at the next conference and take you out to dinner."

"You would promote CrimsonBio? I don't need dinner."

"The dinner is a bonus," he said.

I giggled, and he gave me a brilliant smile with dazzlingly white teeth.

"Blaze, do you ever not flirt?" I moved up with him in line.

"You call it flirting, I call it being charming." He tapped my nose.

"Okay, Mr. Charmer, I accept the bet."

"Here's your pass." The line check attendant handed him a bag. I wore mine already around my neck.

"Yeah, thanks."

"Do we need to do anything else?" I probed, ready to get back to the room so I could study.

"Nope, more direction will be given tomorrow. So tonight you can relax," she replied, and we thanked her and went back to talk and watch the crowd of people fill the room.

"I'm exhausted. I had a long night." I yawned, and he looked down at his watch and nodded.

"We can go back up to the room."

"You don't have to come. I need to talk with the front desk anyway."

"You've had a long day. Sleep in my room and tomorrow you can handle the things with the hotel clerk."

I rubbed the back of my neck nervously. "Are you sure?"

"Yeah, it's no big deal and besides, most hotels are full."

"Oaky, I'll crash the night in your room."

"And the bet?"

We left the Ballroom where they'd hosted the check-in and headed to the elevator back up to the suite.

"If I win you have to promote CrimsonBio."

"And if you lose, you have to have dinner with me."

"So I'm one of many women you'll have on your roster."

He motioned for me to step on the elevator first as the doors opened.

"Dinner and—"

"I knew it ! Always a catch, but I'm not sleeping with you."

"Hold up. Who said anything about sleeping together?"

In the elevator, an older couple who were behind us looked surprised.

"What do you want besides dinner?"

"At the dinner you have to give out business cards from my company to a potential investor."

My jaw clenched in anger at the cockiness of him thinking I would stoop to that level of pettiness.

"That's not fair."

"How is that not fair? You win, I promote CrimsonBio."

"You want a parade of me prancing around about your company," I fussed as we waited for the elevator to ding, and the couple behind us started to leave.

"Honey, he's cute. I'd lose on purpose," the older gray-haired woman suggested.

Of course he heard her as the doors closed, and I rolled my eyes as he rubbed his chin.

"See? It just happens naturally."

"She hasn't met you personally yet."

* * *

I already knew the lengths it would take to win, and distracting me about a bet might be his strategy. Blaze opened the door, and I sauntered in, removed the jacket I'd purchased from the boutique, and slipped my feet out of my heels. Then he shut and locked the door, took his coat off, and headed to the bedroom.

"Think about my bet and find a movie. I'm heading to the shower."

Nodding, I watched as his back muscles flexed, grabbed

my purse, slid my phone out, and saw messages from my family and friends asking how everything was going.

Trisha: Did you get a room?

Trisha: Hello?

Melody: Diego told me he talked to Blaze. I'll see you soon.

Mom: Make sure you wear a bra.

Lord, let me call Trisha back, otherwise she'll continue calling me all night. I dialed her number and waited for her to answer.

"About time, what happened to you?" Trisha queried in annoyance.

"Trying to get settled in the room."

"So did you go to another hotel?"

"Not yet." I whispered over the phone.

"Really! Mr. Blaze must of changed your mind." She purred.

"Trisha, is that all you can think about?"

"I mean, Blaze looks like he has nice taste."

I cackled at her statement. "He does, but I'm not thinking of him in that way," I told her, knowing I would probably pass out if we ever had sex. He looked like he could fuck me into a coma.

"Stop lying to yourself and to me. Where is he now?"

"The shower, and he saw me naked earlier," I blurted out.

"I'm sorry, what?"

"The showerhead blasted me, which caused me to slip and hurt my leg."

"Maybe you need a vacation after this situation."

"The worst trip ever." I slipped the badge off my neck, put it down on the table, gripped the remote, and turned the TV on to a movie channel.

"You get the movie picked out?" he said, walking into the living room wearing only a pair of Nike jogging pants and a T-shirt.

"Damn," I mumbled to myself.

"What was that?" He spread his arms out on the back of the couch. The fresh, crisp smell from his bodywash smelled good and pissed me off at the same time. It reminded me that I had nothing with me except my purse and small items in a carry-on bag full of makeup, medicine, toothbrush, and hair wrap.

"Trisha is on the phone." I shook my phone in his face.

"I can already feel this is going to be a long conversation." He took the remote out of my hands.

"You seem distracted," Trisha giggled through the phone.

"No, I'm not."

"Are you ready for tomorrow?"

"Yeah. He proposed a bet, though."

"Who did?"

"Talk her into taking me up on the bet." Blaze leaned over to my ear and spoke into the phone, and I pushed him back.

"This is a private conversation."

He chuckled and held his hands up. I jumped up and prepared to shower for the night and watch the movie.

"If you need something to sleep in, I have a shirt and shorts on the bed."

"Sounds like your boo making sure you're comfortable," Trisha teased, making kissing noises.

Blaze Newton is my sworn enemy. I said that to myself every time we were in a room together. He oozed sex appeal with his sexy lips, dimples in both cheeks, chestnut skin tone, and washboard abs, which were well-defined in the T-shirt. Our lives would never mesh well together, though, I knew. He was a more upscale, name-brand clothing kind of guy, and I was more of a T-shirt and shorts, eating ice cream on a Friday night type of girl while watching *Golden Girls* reruns. Thirty minutes later, I came out of the bathroom and walked back over to the couch.

"What are we watching?" I queried while I took a call on FaceTime from my cousin Kianna.

"Ohh, put me on FaceTime," Kianna demanded.

"No thank you, and I'll call you tomorrow," I replied.

He turned the channel to see what movie was displayed.

"Looks like *Friday*."

"Man, I haven't seen this in years."

"Me too," I responded while dialing my mother's number. The phone picked up, and I heard loud laughter and music.

"Hello! Hello!"

"Hey, baby, you finally called your mother."

"Hi, Mom, yes, I made it safe. How are things going?"

"Fine. Your father is driving me crazy as usual trying to sneak out to hang with his friends and play cards," Mom huffed. My parents had been married for thirty years and been together for thirty-five. Henry and Jamie Johnston were the fun parents every kid wanted growing up. I was always trying to get them to be serious. Born and raised in California, they did the best they could as young parents, but sometimes, I wanted a firmer structure at home.

"Ava, do you mind if I grab a pillow off the bed?" Blaze inquired.

"Who is that? He sounds sexy," Mom inquired.

A lump caught in my throat.

"Nobody. I'll call you tomorrow, Mom," I answered,

hastily hanging up. I gestured with a nod of my head that it was cool. For the next hour we watched movies on the couch until I fell asleep and woke up in the bed.

* * *

The next day I woke up to two of my bags from my flight in my room. I showered and changed to get the day started and felt like a new person when I came out of the bedroom. Blaze was gone already, and I assumed he was roaming around checking in and getting information for today. Standing in line, I held on to my badge as I waited to be called for an interview. This was my first time being interviewed on TV, and I made sure my favorite blue dress, high heels, and light makeup were on point. The room was full of media and reporters. My eyes glanced at the huge sign on the walls with the name in lights: *America's Next Top Chemist*. This was really happening in real time, a contestant on the highest-rated TV show.

"Hi, Ava, this is Wren, a reporter from CTN news," the producer said as he called me in. I extended my hand for a shake.

"Hi, nice to meet you."

"Ava, you're one of five people competing today. How do you feel?" She pointed the microphone up close with the cameraman behind her.

"It feels weird and fun at the same time. I'm still in disbelief," I replied, tucking a loose strand of hair behind my ear.

"The producers say it's only two women this year and three men. If you don't win, who would you pick to win?" she grilled.

"Good question. I would ask for a recount, because I'm winning today," I joked, and we all laughed.

"Blaze! Over here, Blaze!" she shouted, and I turned to look around as he walked up next to me, placing his hand on the small of my back.

"Blaze Newton, all the ladies want to know, are you single?" Wren flirted, pushing the microphone in his face.

"Wren, you know I don't kiss and tell," Blaze answered with a wide smile at the camera.

She giggled like a high school girl, and her cheeks flushed a warm red. I rolled my eyes at the display and stepped to the side to give them room.

Wren cleared her throat. "So what can we expect out of you two in the competition?"

Blaze motioned for me to answer, and I waved back at him to start first.

"Not to give my secrets away, but I'm showing off what Newton Industries can do when we have the right equipment and time. Our future developments will be revolutionary," Blaze commented.

"I'm very excited to see what you're working on." Wren rested a hand on his arm. I wanted to gag at the display of flirtation she was giving off. I couldn't believe a reporter was acting this way in front of everyone.

"What about you, Ava?" Blaze motioned at me, and a little cocky smirk appeared on his face.

"I'm just here for the snacks," I joked, and she waved her hand around for the camera to cut. Not to be a third wheel, I walked away, heading to the next interview panel; the room held about fifty people, including the staff of the show. Going in the direction of the next reporter, I cut through the line of crewmen as they set up more equipment for the stage. I wasn't paying enough attention to where I was going, and my foot caught in the extension cord. I tripped and pulled the light stand down with me, causing the entire back lighting to go out.

"Fuck!" I shouted, rubbing my hurt right ankle.

"Are you all right?" A staff member rushed over to help me up. He lifted my arm around his neck. I hadn't broken my ankle, thank God, but it did hurt.

"What's going on, Ava?" Abigail, my producer grilled. We each had a producer that we would stay in contact with throughout the taping of the show. Abigail had flown in today and met me down here. I had explained about yesterday, and she was looking into the problem. Right now, I just wanted to give up and fly back home based on all the issues I kept coming across.

"Sorry, I tripped on the cord," I said, dusting off my dress.

"We only have one more interview, then you have free time until dinner. Think you'll make it?" Abigail queried.

"I'll be fine, Abigail."

I put on a brave face, walked to the next reporter, and prepared to answer the same questions as I had with Wren.

"Hi, I'm Johnathan from BAM Network, a proud science channel of all things chemistry and biology and one of the sponsors of this show. Tell me, Ava, what do you expect to gain from this opportunity?" Johnathan quizzed.

"I hope to gain friends, learn from my colleagues, and win the money as a bonus."

"You work for CrimsonBio, correct?"

"I do. My best friend, Melody, started the company, and I work as the director alongside her."

"We'd love to see more women in the industry. What have you done so far on the show?"

"Today is the first day we've been allowed to mix and

mingle, the first day was check-in and tonight is the dinner. From the past, it's been a total of four or five days of competitions if I'm not mistaken."

"Thank you, Ava, for joining us and we look forward to seeing what you come up with on your idea."

Chapter Four

Ava

"Ava, come meet the host, Teddi Finley." Abigail introduced us, and I was awestruck to meet the biggest female biochemist in the business and national host.

"Nice to meet you, Ava." Teddi reached for my hand, but I froze up.

"She is a huge fan," Abigail told her.

"I can tell." Teddi chuckled and patted me on the arm.

"Sorry, I've wanted to meet you for so long," I stuttered.

"No worries. I'm just like you."

"You're one of the main reasons I got into science," I rambled on. A group of reporters approached us.

"What made you want to come here?" she questioned.

"We have to save that for the show, Teddi," Abigail cut in, and I stepped to the side as the makeup artist started to apply makeup on her.

"Maybe we can have a chat later when all of this is over," Teddi muttered.

I nodded and watched her get her mic up and prepare to film. She looked to be in her late forties with light brown skin and long, thick, black hair. Surprisingly, she was shorter than me, around five-six to my five-seven.

"Over here, Ava." Abigail nudged me to a crowd of people in the back corner, and I followed to try and see what had all the attention. I pushed through and saw Blaze in a relay race with another contestant.

"I thought we shouldn't be doing anything until the show airs?" I questioned.

"It's harmless fun."

"All right, so you have to draw different test tubes. Red or blue," Blaze explained.

"You have someone on your team already. I need someone else." The tall, dark-haired guy pushed his glasses up to avoid them falling.

"That's fine, but I get to pick your partner," Blaze told him.

He shrugged.

"Don't let him pick your partner," I blurted out, and everyone went quiet.

Blaze smirked at me.

"Are you in the competition?" the guy quizzed.

I peered at Abigail, and she shoved me forward.

"Uhmmm..."

"She is, and I think you are perfect as his partner," Blaze replied.

"Do you two know each other?" Our eyes met as he gestured between us.

"No." "Yes." Both Blaze and I responded simultaneously.

"Huh?"

"Go ahead, Ava, you'll be fine." Abigail shooed me forward.

"Yeah, it'll be fun. Nothing like losing a little game on

live TV," Blaze remarked. I scoffed, walked up to the table that was near the wall, and picked up the test tube.

"Who said anything about losing?"

"Are you sure you don't know him?"

"I'm positive."

"Why don't we make it interesting?" Blaze challenged, and my ears perked at that statement.

"How?"

"A hundred bucks."

"What? No."

"Yes!" my partner blurted out.

I grasped his arm and pulled him back to whisper in his ear, "Are you crazy? I'm not spending money. I don't know you."

"Don't worry. We got it in the bag." He jerked away and went back to the table. I groaned and stepped back over and waited for the directions to be explained.

"This doesn't count for the show, right?" I probed to make sure.

Abigail shook her head. "No, this is all fun."

"So the way it works is we have to name as many as possible of the blood test tube colors in thirty seconds," Blaze explained.

"That's easy."

"Abigail will watch the clock, and this beautiful lady will hold them up." Blaze held the hand up of some groupie that was standing too close if you asked me. She practically lived in his body by the way she was clinging on to him.

"Don't mess this up."

Having bitten my tongue, I sucked my teeth in response to my partner's demand. "I can hold my own."

"What is your name?" he questioned. He introduced himself as Joel.

"Ava."

"Okay, thirty seconds is ready. On your mark... Go!" Abigail shouted, and the blonde held the first tube up.

"Yellow! Oncology. Blue is hematology," I shouted as my mind went completely blank.

"Biochemistry, endocrinology," Joel added, and we clapped and shook hands in excitement.

"Ten seconds!" Abigail shouted.

"Uhmmm... Pink is...crap."

"I thought you knew your stuff. It's transfusion lab." Joseph shook his head in disappointment.

"Three seconds!" Abigail repeated.

"Purple is laven—"

"That's time!" Abigail interrupted.

"Great! Now we're screwed," Joel grunted.

"All right, Blaze, your turn." Abigail started to set the clock.

"He won't make it, just watch."

He held up a piece of paper, and we all looked at him as he stood there.

"Come on, your time has started," Abigail explained.

"It's right here; the rules didn't say how to name it, just to get it done in thirty seconds," Blaze pointed out.

My mouth opened and closed in helpless fury. I was fuming. "You cheated!"

"Technically, I didn't," Blaze responded, so I snatched the papers from his hands and read them over quickly.

"Why didn't I think of that?" After throwing his hands in the air, Joel reached into his pocket and retrieved some cash.

"I'm not paying him. That's cheating."

"We lost fair and square," Joel said, slapping the money in Blaze's hand.

"Then you pay him." I tried to storm off but felt a hand grip my elbow.

"I won, and you owe me." Blaze crossed his arms over his chest, and I tapped my foot and put a hand on my hip with a scowl.

"You cheated, so I don't owe you anything."

"So you're a sore loser?"

"No I'm not."

"Yeah, pretty much." He sighed, rocking back on his feet.

"I guess your little setup would have worked if I wasn't on to you."

"What are you talking about?"

"The bet... Yep, this was all to get me to agree." I wagged my finger around the room.

He grinned and stepped closer in my face.

"Double or nothing."

"I knew it!" I jumped up and down like a ten-year-old kid that has solved a crime.

He laughed, and I remembered I was wearing a dress and was still in front of cameras. I composed myself and cleared my throat.

"All right, Jessica Lansbury, calm down." He placed a hand on my shoulder.

I knocked it off. "No deal and no fifty dollars."

"Okay, all or nothing."

"Here we go."

"I'll forget about the fifty dollars on one condition."

"What now?"

"If you win the competition, I will donate my resources to CrimsonBio."

"And if you win?"

"You have to come work for me."

I gasped in shock.

* * *

Two hours later, I was back in the room, having finished showering and changing. I wanted to go out and do a little sightseeing before dinner. I was still surprised by Blaze's new stipulation that I work for him. Yes, he had a huge platform, but I could never leave my best friend high and dry like that. I zipped my shorts up and slid my feet into flat sandals and made sure I had my EpiPen with me in case any allergic reactions came up again. I heard the click of the door opening as I walked out of the room, and I saw Blaze coming inside with Melody and Diego behind him.

"OMG! You made it," I shouted and ran toward them.

"Yass, honey. You look so cute, and I need this outfit," Melody told me, tugging on my shorts. We all laughed at her statement.

"Diego! So good to see you," I said as I released Melody and hugged Diego.

"You too, Ava. How is everything going with my boy here?" he quizzed.

"We haven't killed each other so far," I responded, glaring at him.

"Are you heading out somewhere?" Melody probed.

"I was going out to do a little shopping and maybe hit the beach before dinner."

"We'll join you," Melody said.

"Are you sure? Diego is probably tired from the flight and wants to rest."

"I am, babe. Do you mind if I pass on this one?" Diego suggested.

"That's fine. We can have a little girl chat and hit the spa."

"Save the spa for another day; I need to be refreshed for the first day tomorrow," I told her.

Melody pecked Diego on the lips before the door closed behind him, then she looped her arm in mine as we headed to the elevator.

"So tell me what's the deal with you," she demanded.

A nervous smile played along the edge of my lips. "Nothing is going on," I answered.

She shoulder-bumped me. "Blaze and you alone in a hotel suite, and nothing happened?"

"I'm not interested in him, and he's a manwhore anyway," I sassed.

Melody chuckled and shook her head. "You can't judge a man like that, Ava. Besides, they can be reformed with the right woman. Look at Diego now. When we first met two years ago, I never fathomed I would be married to him. Now we're happily married, and hopefully, one day will have kids."

"Yeah, but Diego wanted to settle down and fall in love. How many times have we heard about Blaze in and out of the clubs with women? Girls were fighting over him back in California. That would be too stressful for me," I reminisced as we stepped off the elevator and walked through the hotel lobby. It was a beautiful day on Ocean Drive, people were out, and it wasn't too hot. The fancy cars were driving up and down the street. It gave me old Hollywood-type vibes.

"Let's stop there," I said, pointing to a store just up ahead.

"Blaze is a cool guy once you know him. The women

fighting over him is something I can't explain, but I can tell you that if he's interested, he will make it known."

"Well, good thing he's not interested in me because I'm not interested in him."

I held the door open, and she sauntered in behind me and immediately went to a rack of long, flowy dresses that would be perfect for a day at the beach. Lifting a long, stretchy cream-and-gray dress, I held it up to my body, standing in front of the mirror.

"That would be sexy on you with your hips filling it out." Her usual crooked smile touched her lips.

I arched a questioning eyebrow in her direction. "I don't like that look."

"What look?"

"That look of *buying that dress because you're getting a man out of this trip if it's the last thing I do* look."

"Wow! A simple look said all that?" Melody answered, snatching the dress out of my hands.

"Yes, because I know my friends, and you're brewing something in your mind, and I want you to stop," I whined, stomping my feet.

"Stop acting like a baby and go with the flow, Ava."

A deep frown crossed my brow. I waved to her, ignoring her statement.

"No, Melody, this trip is about winning the money for CrimsonBio and hopefully helping the center. Now help me find something for tonight."

"I like this dress, and we can grab one more as an option, but the first one would be perfect."

I agreed and went to the cash register, and she leaned on the counter next to me. I stared out of the window at all the people having fun skating and sitting in their cars, bumping music.

"I want to try the shoe store I saw on the way here."

"Okay. Did your luggage finally come?"

"Yeah, and I need to question Blaze about that."

"Why?"

I thanked the clerk and grabbed my receipt to leave.

"It was next to his bed this morning."

"Probably the airline contacted the hotel."

"I can give him a little props for being nice about everything."

"You mean with the room."

The room, the food, and the massage on my leg. *Stop thinking about him.*

"He's been a gentleman to some degree."

She pushed the door, and the bell chimed as we strolled into Shoe Palace. Melody pointed at a pair of black boots.

"What does that mean?"

"He cheated earlier today, and I owe him fifty dollars."

"Did you pay him?"

"No." I scoffed and picked up a pair of red heels.

"How did he cheat then?"

I set the shoes near my feet in the mirror to check against my pink toenail polish. For the dinner coming up, I wanted to look sophisticated and sexy at the same time.

"He made up some dumb rule that didn't make sense."

"What was the rule?"

"To name the blood test tube colors in thirty seconds."

"What's wrong with that?"

"We called them out, and he wrote them down on paper."

She burst out in laughter, and I rolled my eyes and crossed my arms, waiting for her to finish. Thinking it over, I decided he'd played the game well.

"Ava, you know that's a genius move, friend," she added, pointing to the silver ankle boots.

I chuckled. "Don't tell him I agree. His head is already big."

"Anything else you've found big?" Melody booty-bumped me.

"No, Melody. You're just like Trisha."

"What did she say?"

"Asked if I had Peter and to do show and tell with Blaze."

"Pussy Popping Peter." Melody rolled her hips in a circle, and I laughed.

"Oh. My. God! Not you too."

"We are here for a few days in Miami. Live it up, girl."

I grabbed the silver ankle boots and red heels and sauntered to the register.

"First the money and then I'll think about having fun."

"Good, maybe you won't need Peter for too long with Blaze around." Melody winked and pulled out her credit card.

"What are you doing?" I blocked her hand.

"I'm paying."

"That will be sixty-two dollars even," the salesclerk said.

"I can pay for myself."

"Stop being stubborn, and this is my treat."

"Melody."

"Ava."

"Ma'am, don't take her money." I reached in my purse to remove my wallet.

"Too late." Melody chuckled, and the woman passed her card back and put the receipt in my bag.

"I can't take you anywhere."

"You'll thank me later."

* * *

Fifteen minutes later, we went into the ice cream shop next door.

"What are you getting?" I quizzed.

"I'll get the strawberry and vanilla swirl," she replied.

Before she could protest, I pulled out my wallet, placed a ten-dollar bill down, and ordered us both a scoop of strawberry swirl. The cashier gave me the change back, and we stepped to the side to wait for our order.

"You're going to be on TV. Are you nervous?" Melody wondered.

"At first I was, but then I knew what it could do for the company and hiring more people and doing research with updated equipment, so it's a No-brainer for me."

"The first statement is tomorrow, and you guys do a competition or what?"

"Funnily enough, it's like all the other reality shows on TV. Except we have white coats on, and we present our goal, and they break it down into groups and then the final individual."

"Number twenty-one!" the cashier said.

"Only the person and no help, right?" She took the ice cream off the counter when our number was called.

We slumped down into the chairs.

"Yep, one of the reasons I needed you here for moral support is to make sure all of my calculations are correct. I have everything locked in my bag."

"That's good. Just imagine if you win that money. I can see so much improvement for the company."

"It's time we updated our computer systems, get more staff hired, and added more researchers."

"I agree."

"Good. What are you wearing to dinner tonight?"

"I'm not sure, and I have about three ideas."

From behind, I heard that same familiar laugh and felt his presence before he entered.

"I knew we'd find you two here. Scoot over, baby," Diego said as he bent down to kiss her lips. Blaze tapped Diego on the shoulder.

"You want anything?"

"Yeah. Milkshake." Diego nodded.

"I'll grab yours, Diego," Blaze said.

"What happened to giving us girls time and you taking a nap?" Melody questioned. I tried to avoid not staring, I cleared my throat.

Blaze was wearing jeans that showcased he was packing something large, and the thin, gray shirt played up his broad shoulders and six-pack.

"I missed you, and Blaze wanted to get out of the room. Ava, I put fifty dollars on you winning the bet," Diego stated, taking a Spoonful of Melody's ice cream.

"What bet?" Melody looked between Diego and me as Blaze sat down next to me, brushing against my shoulder. He passed Diego a milkshake. I scooted over to give us space in the booth and ran a hand across my forehead in aggravation. If we weren't in public in a group setting, I would have kicked Blaze under the table for telling Diego about the bet.

"Blaze thinks he can beat me in the competition, and he suggested we bet."

"If she wins, I will pull resources for CrimsonBio at the next conference and take her out for dinner," Blaze explained, lifting the straw to his lips. Melody grinned and clapped her hands together in excitement, and I groaned, already knowing she wasn't going to like the other side of the bet.

"What do you get, Blaze, if you win?" she probed.

I closed my eyes and waited for the pin to drop.

"Ava has to promote Newton Industries and go as my date to my cousin's wedding." I glared at him, not remembering that part of the deal.

"Where's your cousin's wedding?" I questioned.

"Jamaica," he stated nonchalantly.

"What!" I yelled in shock.

Melody and Diego bent over in laughter, and I wanted to slap them both for thinking this was funny. No way in hell would I agree to this type of bet. Bad enough he lied and didn't tell her about me working for him. No, sir, being alone with Blaze in Jamaica was a no-go. I suddenly felt hot and nervous and waved my hand to stop the excitement.

"I never agreed to that," I snapped, sitting back in my chair.

"You seem to be scared you'll lose the bet, Ava. Are you chickening out?"

"Jamaica this time of year would be nice. Maybe Diego and I should go with you guys. Not to the wedding, but for the trip itself," Melody responded, grabbing the milkshake out of Diego's hand.

"Really, Melody, you're supposed to be on my side with me fighting for your company."

"At least you get a free trip out of it," Diego implied.

I rose up, pulled my shorts down from rising up my thighs, and grabbed my trash to head back to the hotel.

All three of them followed behind me as they continued joking at my expense.

"Think about the men you'll meet in Jamaica, Ava," Melody commented.

"Hold up now, Melody; this trip is about my cousin's wedding. Not Ava trying to get her groove on like Stella," Blaze remarked.

Melody waved him off, and I laughed, thinking about the opportunity to actually meet a guy. The dating scene had been a bit scarce for the past few years, and I had my on-call type of guys when I was feeling in the mood to have sex. But most of them were wrapped up in their own lives and not able to stay on track with being consistent. The biggest pet peeve of mine is a guy that can't communicate and is not consistent. Diego held the door open for us, and we all walked back into the hotel and toward the elevators. My room debacle was still playing heavily on my mind, but I would let Abigail handle that. I didn't have to pay for the room, but the principle of having the contestants bumped for some high-profile guests was insane.

"What time is dinner?" Melody queried.

"We have an hour to get ready and be back down there," I answered and hopped on the elevator with Blaze behind, grasping the side of my waist to keep me from stubble over. He hit the button for the suite, and Diego and Melody pushed the floor for their room. They were on the level below us, and they got off first. It was awkward for a second until the doors opened, and we shuffled to the door.

"I'm not going to Jamaica with you."

"We'll see," Blaze countered, shutting the door.

"Whatever, Blaze," I responded, trying to get the last word.

"I know what you're doing, Ava, and it won't work."

I avoided eye contact.

"What am I doing? Please enlighten me."

He slid a hand in his pocket and stared into my eyes.

"That little pout on your face will get you in trouble," he insisted and shifted his body, walking away from me to the bedroom.

"What does that mean?" Again, I couldn't leave well enough alone and began to follow but stopped when someone knocked on the door. It was Melody with my bags.

"You forgot these." Melody held them out.

"Thanks, my brain is on overdrive with the competition, and I forgot."

"Sure, it's just the show and not the roommate that's taking you to Jamaica," Melody teased, poked me in my side.

"I'm positive it's the show and nothing else. Are you guys meeting me downstairs or here in the room?" I quizzed her to change the topic.

"We can meet downstairs," Melody answered. I again thanked her, then closed the door to head to the bedroom. When I accidentally bumped into a hard, muscular chest, which felt like a brick wall, he caught me. Before I could fall, he wrapped his arms around my waist to pull me close to him.

"Umm, thanks." I glanced into his eyes, licking my lips unconsciously.

"Ava, have you always been this clumsy?" His hand rested on my lower back as he probed.

I had trouble speaking because the elongated, thick member between us twitched, almost causing me to come on myself. *Why am I attracted to cocky, big-dicked, egomaniac men?* Blaze removed his arms as he bent to pick up his suit.

"I have."

"What type of dress did you get for tonight?"

"A simple dress Melody helped me pick out. Nothing to call home about," I joked.

"Cool, I'll let you get ready first. I know you women like to be in the bathroom all night," Blaze stated as he let me go around him.

"I'm not that bad."

Chapter Five

Blaze

I couldn't take my eyes off her all night. I tried to keep my distance, but it was getting harder to do. She infuriated me so much, and at the same time, she was delicate, sweet, headstrong, and sexy—all the things my mother would love in a woman for me. Except that settling down was the last thing on my mind at the moment. Winning the prize money and growing my business even bigger was my plan. I couldn't let anything distract me from that. The bet of her coming to the wedding was something last minute after I talked with my cousin. I needed a date and for sure wasn't asking any of the women I'd dealt with in the past. Melody and Diego stood next to me, talking with another contestant for the show. All of the producers and staff were here. The cameras were off tonight, so we could all mix and mingle. Ava came over with a big smile on her face. Her hair was up in a high bun on top of her head, and her dress, an off-white or cream-colored long sleeveless dress with a split on the side, fit her like a glove. I liked that she was wearing very little makeup. Her features were soft and subtle.

"You look gorgeous, Ava," Melody complimented her, reaching for a hug.

"Thank you, and you two look amazing." Ava waved her finger from Melody to Diego.

"What about me?" I queried.

"You look all right," Ava said dryly, and I shook my head.

"Ava, we haven't met. I'm Cody Sampson. Another contestant for the show," Cody held his palm out. He was a little shorter than me, short buzz cut and slim built.

"Hi, nice to meet you, Cody. What company are you playing on behalf of?" Ava probed.

"Dexter Laboratories. It's a company based out of New York City," Cody replied.

"Nice," Ava responded.

"Ladies and gentlemen, you can take your seats; food will be delivered shortly," the announcer explained. I led Ava to the table they had sectioned off for each group. We happened to be sitting together. I had Melody and Diego placed next to us and pulled out her chair.

"Thanks," Ava said.

"You're welcome, and you do look beautiful."

"Thank you."

"I knew that was you over here. How are you, Blaze?" I heard a squeaky voice yell. I groaned and put my head in my hands. I didn't expect to run into one of my biggest mistakes. Sharon Langford and I had slept together once five years ago, and she was still to this day trying to get me to take her out again. How she could even think I'd go back again, not only because she was terrible and couldn't last long and complained throughout the encounter about how she didn't expect me to be that big. But especially given the lapse of time between our only encounter was beyond me. But who knows how women think?

"Yoo hoo! Blaze darling, it's me." Sharon rested her hand on my shoulder.

"I think she's talking to you," Melody covered her mouth and whispered.

I clenched my teeth together and peered over at Sharon.

"Sharon, hey. What's up?"

She grinned and bent down to kiss me, but I leaned away.

"Hold up! I'm taken." I barked out the first thing that came to mind. I remembered her constantly calling and texting me right afterward to have a second chance. Not up for playing games, I'd blocked her and gone on with my life.

"Stop lying, silly."

"I'm not lying. This is my girlfriend." I grasped Ava's hand and kissed the back of it.

She spit out her champagne across the table and almost choked.

"Girlfriend!" Ava shouted, drawing all eyes to our table.

I smiled and wrapped my hand around her waist, whispering in her ear, "Play along."

"Why should I?" she hissed, smiling to not draw attention.

"Because you owe me."

She tried to jerk away. "Let me go. I don't owe you."

"The room, your bags."

That seemed to calm her down for a second.

"Nope."

"Ava, just do me this favor."

Ava looked behind me. I glanced at Sharon, and she waved at me.

"She doesn't seem like your type."

"And what's my type?"

"Big boobs like the blonde the other day."

"What do you want?"

"Call off the bet that I never agreed to in the first place."

"You must feel like you're going to lose. Not confident?" I taunted her.

"That reverse psychology doesn't work on me."

I sighed and rubbed a hand down my face.

"Okay, pretend to be my girlfriend and I'll call off half the bet."

"You're not slick."

"I really need someone for Jamaica, you did sleep in my suite, and I bought you dinner."

She groaned. "You're paying for Jamaica?"

"Blaze!" Sharon called out.

I turned.

"One second!" I held up my index finger. "I'm paying for Jamaica, everything."

"All I have to do is pretend to be your girlfriend tonight."

"I thought you'd be happy to see me. I'm the judge of the show," Sharon explained.

"For the rest of the show?" A crease formed between my brows

"Considering my expertise is working with World Science, I was chosen to be a judge." In the middle of the conversation, Sharon placed a hand on my chest.

Ava rolled her eyes, then put on the biggest fake smile I've ever seen.

"Hi I'm Ava, Bla...Blaz...Blaze's girlfriend." Her hand extended to Sharon as she stuttered.

"Really? When did that happen?" Sharon inquired.

"Tonight," Ava answered.

"What she means is it feels like a new love every night, but we've been together for a year," I explained, wrapping a hand around Ava's waist.

"Oh, she doesn't seem like your type," Sharon commented.

"What's his type exactly?" Ava's face scrunched up in anger.

"I mean you're cute, for the sister type," Sharon suggested, and I could feel heat off Ava's glare, her nails digging into my hand.

"How about we sit down and eat?"

"Yeah, let's eat."

"Maybe you should eat a salad tonight, sweetie. You know the camera adds ten pounds." Sharon flipped her hair and turned back to the stage, walking off.

Ava tried to lunge at her, and I bear-hugged her from behind, walking back to the table.

"Lucky you grabbed Ava, because I was ready to pound your little friend in the ground." Melody fussed, dropping her napkin on the table.

"Who was that?" Diego wondered.

"One of the judges for the show and someone I know."

"Someone you slept with," Ava hissed, jerking out of my hold.

"One time we slept together."

The waitstaff came to our table and poured more champagne. The music went low, and the MC on the stage started to speak.

"Obviously she has a difference of opinion."

"Sharon is harmless."

"Ladies and gentlemen, I want to introduce our judges for the competition." Teddi's words came through the microphone.

"The way she's staring at you, Ava, I'd watch out for her." Melody tilted her head toward the stage. I glanced at the three judges, and Sharon was the only one with a harsh mug on her face.

"I better not lose this competition over your little dick." Ava pointed at my crotch, and I shifted in the chair.

"We both know it's not little."

Melody looked intrigued. "When did this happen?"

"It didn't," replied Ava.

"You are married, so why ask about his sex life?" Diego growled, and Melody brushed him off and sat down next to Ava.

"We haven't slept together."

"Well, isn't it nice to see the cheater and the cheapskate." Joel walked up to our table, eating a shrimp puff.

"Who is that?" Melody pointed at him.

"No one!" Ava and I answered at the same time.

Joel wiped his hands on his pants and reached out to shake Melody's hand.

"I'm Joel, a contestant on the show."

"Nice to meet you, Joel."

"He's mad Blaze scammed him out of a hundred dollars." Ava reached for a piece of bread and butter.

"Which you still owe me half," Joel hinted.

"I don't owe you anything." Ava bit into her bread once again.

"Joel, do you mind having a private conversation?"

"We have Danny Myers, the late nineties rock star from The Myers band that created the song for our show," Teddi announced.

"Actually I want my money from her." He pointed at Ava, who continued eating her bread and butter.

"Next we have the lovely and fabulous Sharon Langford, retired science maven who helped create the World of Science channel." Teddi introduced the second judge.

"Not retired, dear." Sharon grabbed the microphone from her hand.

"Oh, well, it says 'retired' on the card." Teddi held up the card to show.

Sharon had been fired from the World of Science channel for inflating the budgets and spending money on herself. I met her at a work conference a few times, flirted, and we'd gone out for drinks and ended up at a hotel. The rest was a nightmare.

Teddi grabbed the microphone back.

"Whatever," Sharon sassed, smiling for the cameras.

"For our final judge, Carl Clinton, the owner of StemI, a tech brand that functions to bring all the latest science information, and humanitarian." Teddi clapped her hands as he waved to the crowd. The crowd cheered, and I was ready for this night to be over and away from Sharon.

"Joel, here, take the money back." I reached in my pocket and gave him back the hundred dollars.

"What's the catch?"

I clapped him on the back and walked him away from the table.

"No catch, just want to make sure we're square."

"Cool." Joel smiled and went over to the tray of shrimp the waitress was holding.

"Blaze!" Sharon blocked me.

"We shouldn't be talking."

"Why? There's nothing wrong with a friendly chat." Sharon leaned against my chest.

"There is when he has a girlfriend." Ava arrived next to me and linked her hand with mine.

"Amy, right?" Sharon stood tall, clasping her hands together.

"Ava."

I cleared my throat.

"Yeah, right."

"Sharon, if you'll excuse me, I need to tend to my girlfriend."

"Sure, but I need to speak with you about the competition," Sharon told me.

"What about it?"

"It's private."

"Shouldn't you talk to all of us if it concerns the competition?" Ava brought up a good point.

"I agree with Ava. We wouldn't want you to be seen as cheating."

"Sharon! Sharon! We need you for photos." Teddi looked out into the crowd.

"She's right here!" I yelled, pointing at her.

"We will continue this conversation later." Sharon switched her hips and went back to the stage. Ava dropped my hand, stormed back to the table, grabbed her purse, and hugged Melody goodbye.

"I'll see you tomorrow," Melody responded as she let her go.

"I will, cross my fingers." Ava waved at Diego, and I decided to finish my dinner and hang out with my friends. Tomorrow was the first day's challenge, and I felt confident in my skills to win and prepare for the grand prize.

Chapter Six

Ava

I rinsed my mouth out, slipped on my hair wrap, washed the last remnants of makeup off, and checked myself out in the mirror wearing a short camisole set and rabbit slippers. Today was draining, but it had been fun to spend time with Melody. Now I just needed to get a good night's rest before tomorrow's challenge, and even with Sharon giving me the evil eye, my chances of winning the money were high.

Ring! Ring!

I looked out of the bathroom door and saw my cell ringing on the bed. I ran to answer and saw Trisha's name scrolled across. I answered and heard loud laughter in the background.

"Hello?"

"The queen of the ball finally answered," Kianna blurted out, and I pulled the phone away from my ear and saw they had set up a three-way call.

"Do you two know what time it is?" I fussed, spreading out on the bed and leaning against the headboard.

"We do, and Kianna just got back from the radio event," Trisha said.

Kianna worked at a radio station and wanted to get a lead promoter position. She'd worked there for over two years. She knew a lot of musicians and was hip to everything that was going on in the music business.

"How was the event?" I quizzed.

"Fine, but tell us how it's going in Miami," Kianna questioned.

"We had the cast dinner tonight in the ballroom. Melody and Diego came down."

"What are the other contestants like?" Trisha probed.

I yawned, leaned over the bed to grab Peter out of my bag, and placed it on the nightstand.

"I only met one or two people. A guy named Joel is annoying."

"Why?" they inquired at the same time.

"Because he says I owe him fifty bucks. It's a long story."

"How are things with Blaze?"

"All right, I guess."

"Who's Blaze?" Kianna inquired.

"Nobody."

"Her crush," Trisha said.

"My focus is the competition. Men are the last thing on my mind."

"Men, fine, but Blaze isn't just some guy."

"Spill the beans."

"Nothing to talk about. He was there, and I pretended to be his girlfriend." I mumbled the last part.

The phone went silent.

"Wait, you pretended to be his girlfriend?"

I groaned and turned to lie on my stomach.

"Nothing serious. He just needed me to help him out for a second."

"Why?"

"I guess an ex is a judge of the show."

"Hold up."

"It's fine, not as bad as him taking me to Jamaica," I calmly blurted out.

"What!" Trisha shouted.

"Repeat what you just said slowly," Kianna said.

I blew out a breath.

"He basically bet me if I win he'll promote CrimsonBio."

"Okay, how does Jamaica fit?"

"Let me finish."

"You're not giving us much," Kianna spat.

She called me out as usual. I sometimes ramble on giving small bits of the story, but I hated bringing this up again.

"If he wins I have to go with him to his cousin's wedding in Jamaica."

"Is he paying?" Trisha questioned.

"Does that matter?" I hissed.

Definitely!" the two of them answered.

"Can we talk about something else?" I yawned on the phone.

"Have you used Peter yet?" Trisha inquired.

"No, my mind has been on other things, but I have him for tonight." I smiled, reaching to pick up my vibrator.

"Good, clean out the cobwebs," Kianna joked.

"Oh whatever. I'll call you guys tomorrow after the competition."

"Have fun, and tell Peter I have his cousin over here: Tingly Tommy."

"Bye, you guys."

I chuckled and ended the call, dropping the phone on the bed. Turning Peter to the second highest range, I removed my shorts and lay on my back, resting it against my lips.

"Mmmmm...ssss." I moaned, feeling my honey nectar start to cover the sheets.

I bit my bottom lip, thinking of Blaze's strong arms wrapped around me from earlier and picturing him kissing me along my neck and behind my ear.

"Ugh...Peter!" I cried out.

The door burst open.

"Who is Peter?" Blaze shouted.

"Arghhh! Get out." I dropped the vibrator and rolled off the bed, reaching for the comforter to cover myself up.

"Shit! Sorry." Blaze chuckled, walked in closer, and lifted my vibrator off the bed.

"What are you doing? Get out."

He looked toward the open bathroom door and back at me. The scowl on his face was unreadable.

"This is Peter?" He titled the vibrator sideways.

"You're an asshole. Drop it and get out." I pointed at the door.

"Sorry, I thought you had someone in my room." He dropped it back on the bed. I reached over and grabbed it and walked to the bathroom. I slid my shorts back on.

"Abigail will have my room ready tomorrow."

"Good. I need my privacy back."

"Oh, so you can bring your girlfriend Sharon up here."

He waved me off and went to sit on the bed.

"What are you doing?"

He looked down and jumped up, remembering the sheets held my juices.

"She's not my girlfriend."

"I don't care." I removed the sheets and grabbed another set to change the bed.

"You didn't sound like you were doing it right," he mumbled.

"Get out!"

He laughed and rubbed his chin.

"The bet is still on." He started to walk out of the bedroom.

"I can't wait to win that money," I growled.

"Maybe I'll purchase you a lifetime supply when I win the game prize. You'll have a peter for every day of the week. Even holidays." He winked his left eye and shut the door of the bedroom.

I held the pillow up to my face and screamed.

* * *

It was humid outside for the most part, the music was blasting. Cameras being set, lights shining bright, people roaming around tried to get things in place. I sat in the makeup chair while getting done up for the first competition and watched Joel and the other contestants go through rehearsal. I'd already gone over the structure of the first competition and saw it could be an easy win for me. Besides, Blaze was my biggest competition. The audience was piling in to be directed, and Abigail approached wearing a headset and holding a note pad in her hand. Surprisingly, she was around my age, petite, with a short brown bob and a tawny skin tone.

"Here's your room key. Sorry about the confusion."

I smiled and took it out of her hand.

"A suite?" My eyebrows lifted in surprise.

She nodded.

"The hotel apologized and upgraded your regular room."

"I can't take that." I tried to give it back to her.

"No, you're fine. Besides, it's the hotel's fault. Are you excited?"

"Excited, but nervous." I twisted my hand left to right.

"Everyone gets like that the first time on camera."

"Can I ask you a question?"

"Sure. Hold one second."

I looked down at the key.

"Have Joel standing on the right side." Abigail spoke into the walkie.

"What do you think of the judges?"

"Their production wanted to bring in fresh faces for the new season."

"Sharon Langford."

"What about her?"

"She's very—"

"Snobbish, stuck-up bitch."

I nodded. "Yep."

"I don't have a say in the judges, but I think you have a great chance."

"Thanks."

"Remember why you're here." She patted my shoulder.

"Everybody on set!" A member of the production staff called over the microphone for us to report to the stage. In person, it was much smaller. Various science words were displayed in black and gray. It was like the stage of jeopardy but arranged so we were facing each other, and the host was in the middle.

"Five minutes before we start!" he repeated, and Blaze was told to stand opposite of me, next to Joel. I shook hands with an older woman, Kimberly, who was competing.

"Are you ready for this?" she questioned.

"Yes, how about you?"

"This is my second time getting picked. I'm playing for my students." She pointed to the crowd of kids in the stands.

"That's awesome," I muttered, facing forward. The name of the game in reality TV shows is the story you have and how compelling it is to the audience. It being her second time on the show and backed by students could work in her favor and put me out of the running in the judges' eyes. Bad enough it was her second time chosen.

"All right, everybody, the show is about to start."

Teddi walked up on stage holding a microphone. The countdown began from five, and I started to put on the biggest smile, standing tall with my shoulders back.

"America, are you ready?" Teddi called out to the audience.

"Yesss!!!!" Cheers and excitement were heard throughout the room.

"Everyone in the audience and at home. I'm Teddi Finley, and welcome to a new season of *America's Next Top Chemist*."

There was clapping and high-fives, and we waved to the crowd as the camera panned toward us.

"Today we have three new judges that you know and love. Let's get our judges out here!" Teddi motioned for the judges to walk out. Sharon led them in waving and went to sit down at the table in front of the audience.

"We have Sharon Langford with us. Give her a big hand!" Teddi explained.

"Thank you, Teddi. So happy to be here with you all."

Sharon stared right at Blaze. I rolled my eyes at her blunt flirting in front of everybody.

"She's desperate," I murmured.

"What was that?" Kimberly probed.

The camera was caught in front of my face, and my eyes went wide, like a deer caught in headlights.

"Oh, I see one of our contestants is ready to go."

I held my hands up to say no.

"The competition will start soon, Ava. But let's introduce our next judge, Danny Myers, an amazing singer and songwriter," Teddi went on.

"Thank you, Teddi. Extremely happy to be here with you all and the judges," Danny replied.

"Anytime, Danny. For our final judge, we have Carl Clinton, a humanitarian who is donating the prize money."

"I speak for all the judges when we say this is an amazing show that's supporting future generations," Carl remarked.

"Thank you, judges. So let's meet our contestants." Teddi started to approach our side of the room. I rubbed my sweaty hands on my pants.

"First we have Kimberly. Tell us, Kimberly, who are you playing for?" Teddi questioned, pushing the mic to her.

"I'm playing for my students. This would be great to help take back to our school in Wyoming." Kimberly smiled and waved at the camera.

"I saw a few of them in the audience. Let's get them on camera." Teddi motioned for the camera guy to move in on the audience.

"I'm going to wipe the floor with everybody," Kimberly whispered in my ear.

Teddi turned toward me and grinned.

"Our next contestant. Ava Johnston, who are you playing for?"

I cleared my throat.

"For my best friend and boss Melody at CrimsonBio."

"CrimsonBio is one of the primer labs," Teddi said.

"Yes, I'm very lucky to work there and will use some of the money to keep us going."

"Good for you. Now who do we have over here?" Teddi went to the guy next to me, then across the stage to Blaze's section.

"Now we all know who you are, Mr. Blaze."

Blaze extended his palm out, grasped Teddi's hand, and kissed the back of her knuckle. I clenched my teeth. Our eyes met, and I gripped the buzzer, ready to get started.

"Oh, he's good," Kimberly taunted.

"Teddi, you're looking lovely today."

"Stop it, Blaze. You can't flirt with me, sir."

He held a hand over his heart.

"I would never compromise you, Teddi, unless you ask me to." He kissed her again on the back of her hand.

"Joel, you're up next. What do you have for America?"

Joel reached to kiss her hand, but she jerked back.

"Sorry, I'm nervous. My hands are sweaty," Joel said, rubbing his hands on his pants.

"That's okay. We're going to get started now on *America's Next Top Chemist!*" Teddi yelled out, the music came on, and the director called a break.

"Great job, everyone. Take a breather. You're doing fine." Abigail went to stand next to Teddi.

"We're coming back in five minutes!" a production assistant informed us.

"We're going right into this first game relay race group— elephant toothpaste," Abigail said.

The ingredients were pulled out on rolling trays with protective gear, and they motioned for us to stand together in groups. There were three on each side of the table.

"The first group to finish wins the first challenge."

"You ready?" Kimberly questioned, pulling on gloves.

"Born ready." I put on my goggles.

"Welcome back to *America's Next Top Chemist*. Our first challenge is a relay race for our contestants." Teddi spoke into the camera.

"Wooohooo!!!!" the crowd screamed.

"The group that wins is free from elimination."

"Booo!!"

"Let's get started and set the clock. On the mark you have to run from your table and work as a team. Are we ready, contestants?"

"Yes!" we all screamed loudly.

"Go!" Teddi screamed. The clock began to tick down as I grabbed the bottles and vases. Kimberly picked up the chemicals, and the other teammate got the warm water and dish soap. I kept an eye on the clock as I mixed the peroxide.

"Ready for the yeast?" Kimberly probed, and I nodded.

"Hurry!" I shouted.

"Done!"

My head turned toward the noise, and I saw Teddi running over to Blaze's team.

"Time, we have a winner," Teddi yelled out.

"Of course he wins," Kimberly grumbled, dropping her gloves on the counter.

Chapter Seven

Blaze

I had to give it to him: Joel was good for something. He worked quickly and moved in sync with me. Teddi checked that everything in our blue experiment had been used correctly.

"Congrats! We have the first challenge winners. We'll be right back," Teddi told the camera.

To hear those words made me feel good about the next two challenges if they were like this.

"Tell us, Joel, how are you feeling about winning today?" she probed him, and I stood back, letting him have this shine.

"It was perfect because we knew right off the bat, before it started how to work everything to keep the time down," Joel explained.

"Great job. And how about you, Blaze?"

"Same as Joel. It was a no-brainer, and I can't wait for the next thing."

"Sounds like a challenge to me, audience." Teddi clapped her hands.

"Blaze! Blaze!"

I waved as they called my name.

"We'll be right back with our first elimination," Teddi said.

"Okay, team one, you'll come up here and stand before the judges," Abigail directed Ava's team. I'd hoped she would get kicked off the first day, because it would be too easy to win without a real opponent.

"It's time to hear from our judges on the first elimination."

The crowd got quiet and moved in close as the spotlight was put on Danny.

"Danny, what do you have to say for team one?"

"It looked like they weren't communicating like team two."

"Carl, would you say the same thing?"

"Communication could have been better, and it seemed like Kimberly was nervous." Carl held up his cards with notes.

"To me, Kimberly seemed on top of things, but Ava wasn't as present," Sharon explained.

Ava's jaw clenched, and I knew Sharon was doing this for personal reasons, to make her look bad and get Ava off the show. Teddi's lips pursed together.

"I mean it was obvious if she would have strategized early, like Blaze." Sharon grinned at me.

"So the first person that's going to be eliminated is...? We'll be right back with the results." Teddi pointed at the camera, and the crowd clapped in sync.

Ava started to storm off. Abigail grasped her arm, and it seemed like they were arguing.

"Who do you think they'll knock off?" Joel quizzed.

"I don't know." I sighed and rubbed my chin.

"My money is on your girlfriend," Joel said.

"She's not my girlfriend."

"The way you're staring at her could have fooled me, but you might want to quit because that Sharon babe is throwing daggers at your head."

I glanced to my left and saw Sharon staring back at me. The lights went live, and everyone got into place and prepared for the final moments.

"Ladies and gentlemen, we're back with the results of the first vote of elimination." Teddi held the envelope in her hand.

"YaYa!!!"

Teddi held her hand up to quiet them down.

"The first person eliminated is Andy Yates," Teddi read from the card. His head dropped in disappointment, and he hugged Kimberly and Ava before waving goodbye.

"Ava and Kimberly, you are safe. Please go back to your section," Teddi told them.

Ava smiled and thanked the crowd.

"That is our show for today. We will bring you more next time on *America's Next Top Chemist*."

"Cut!" the director yelled. Staff ran over and started to remove our microphones, and security was standing nearby to make sure no one ran over toward us as the judges were being escorted off the stage.

"Great job, but this doesn't make us friends, you know." As Joel extended his hand, I shook it.

"No hard feelings."

He marched off the set, and the producer was talking with Sharon near the exit as I started to pass by them with security.

"Hey, Blaze, can we talk?" Sharon questioned.

"What's going on, Sharon?"

She tried to interlock her hands with mine, but I politely slid them in my pockets.

"You did great out there today." She pretended to ignore my standoffish demeanor.

"Thanks."

"We're going to dinner. Do you want to join us?" She pointed at the judges.

"I don't think that would be a good idea."

"Why not?"

"I'm a contestant."

Sharon planted her hand on her hip.

"Tell me the real deal with you and her." Sharon motioned to Ava, who was stepping into the cast van to head back to the hotel.

"Last time I'm going to say this, we slept together once."

"So you've never thought about us together?"

"No."

"I didn't mean anything to you?"

"Sharon, it was one night. Let it go."

"But I think we'd be good together." Sharon stepped into my personal space.

"Obviously that night meant more to you than it did to me, but I've moved on."

"Fine. I'm Sharon Langford. I've never begged a man in my life." Sharon jutted her chin in the air, flipped her hair, and switched to the security limo, waiting for the judges to climb in and leave.

Teddi approached me. "Be careful," she warned.

Rubbing my neck, I nodded.

"Great job today."

"Thanks."

"Some of the contestants are getting together at the hotel."

"To hang out?"

"Yeah, and I heard Joel asking Abigail if they could."

"I might stop over."

"You should. You're becoming a fan favorite."

"I'd rather just win the money."

"Keep up the good work and that charm. Something is bound to fall in your lap."

* * *

An hour later, once I made it back to the hotel, I showered and changed my clothes. I met up with Diego and told him about the get-together in Joel's room. He told Melody, who was hanging with Ava already in the room. I heard the loud music and knocked on the door and waited for him to answer. The door opened, and Joel held a red cup in his hand and waved for us to enter. I saw a few of the production staff hanging out.

"This man is toasted."

Joel leaned against the wall, trying to flirt with Kimberly. She looked more annoyed than anything.

"Hey, baby." Melanie walked up to Diego and kissed him on the lips as she wrapped her arms around his neck.

"What's up, Melody?" I gave her a hug.

"You did good today," Melody replied.

"Thanks. Where's Ava?"

Melody waved to the balcony.

"How's her mood?"

"Calm now, but tread lightly when she sees Sharon talking to you."

"That was nothing."

"She thinks Sharon has it out for her."

"Sharon's harmless."

"Well, if she tries to come for her again, I might have to have words with her."

"All right, Mohammed Ali," I joked, heading outside to talk to her on the balcony.

I grabbed a beer off the table and I slid the door open and shut it behind me.

"Melody, I'm fine."

"That's good to know, but you may want to keep an eye on Melody."

Ava turned to face me against the railing. I stood on the wall with my left leg propped up on it.

"What are you doing here?"

"Since I'm a part of the show, Teddi told me about Joey throwing this for everybody to hang out."

"He's starting to grow on me," Ava quipped, turning back around.

"So you're here fighting for CrimsonBio." I marched toward the railing and stood a few feet away from her, facing Flagler Street.

"Yeah." She drank from the red cup.

"What are you drinking?"

"Red wine."

I nodded.

"I'm glad you didn't get cut today." I lifted the beer bottle to my lips.

She blew out a breath and chuckled.

"Thanks, I guess."

"Sharon was wrong for what she said to you."

"Sharon is trying to win you more than judge the contest."

"Well, I'm not interested in her."

"Why did you two break up?"

"That's the thing. We were never together."

"Oh, yeah, she couldn't handle your big dick." She giggled.

I choked on my drink at her outburst.

"How do you know it's big?"

She cursed under her breath.

"Hey, my people. What rocked it out today?" Joel stretched his arms around both our shoulders.

"Joel, you're drunk," Ava said.

Joel snorted. "I'm celebrating."

"Is there food?" I investigated.

"Yep. I asked production if we could order outside of the hotel tonight."

"Is that Kimberly going through someone's wallet?" I lied, pointed at Kimberly while she slid her jacket on to leave.

"What! I'm being robbed. I knew it was a bad idea to come here alone." Joel tripped. I helped him up, and he stumbled back inside of the living room.

"He's way past drunk."

"You know, we are not that much different."

"What do you mean?"

"I'm fighting for this money to help my company."

"I get that, it's just—"

"What?"

"Nothing."

"No, tell me."

"I just have this dream about one day having multiple CrimsonBio labs around the world and internationally."

"That can still happen."

"I doubt it since I lost the first challenge."

"You just need to loosen up."

"You should probably say that to Sharon," Ava cracked.

"Ha, ha. Not funny."

"You're scared of her, aren't you?" She pointed at me.

"What? No."

"Yes you are. Mr. Blaze Newton is scared of a woman." She snickered, covering her mouth.

I stood up and backed her into the corner, when I felt my phone vibrate. I reached in my pocket and pulled it out to see a message from Kenya.

Kenya: Hey, are you back from Miami?

I bit my bottom lip.

"Let me guess. Not Sharon this time." Ava started to walk around me.

"Not what you think."

"We're not an item. Hell, I can barely stand you."

Her comment pissed me off, and I don't know why.

"That goes both ways."

Ava scoffed and marched back into the room, and I chewed on my bottom lip and returned a text to Kenya.

Me: No still in Miami.

Kenya: When you're back lets talk.

Me: I'm going to Jamaica.

I technically didn't lie, but I am going to Jamaica, just not right after Miami.

Kenya: Why are you going to Jamaica?

"What did you do to Ava?" Diego questioned.

"Nothing, why do you ask?"

"She's in there pretty much calling you every name in the book to Melody, which means I'm not getting any sex or sleep tonight." Diego smacked me on the back of the head.

"Ouch! Why'd you hit me?"

"Because your stupid ass is always blocking me form having sex, just like in college."

"You should be thanking me for Sheila's situation."

Me: Busy, can't talk.

I quickly slipped my phone into my pocket.

"That's true, because I could have ended up with three or four kids," Diego joked.

"That was Kenya," I muttered, watching to make sure no one was looking at us.

"I thought that was a little fun thing, nothing serious."

"It's not serious, but Ava caught an attitude."

"Boy, you have more women problems for a man that ain't got a woman."

"Fuck you, Diego." I chuckled.

"True shit."

I could feel my stomach growling.

"Let me get out of here and head to my suite. Now that I have my bed back, I can sleep peacefully."

"Ava told us she finally got a room."

"Yeah, thank God. The girl snores like crazy."

"Hell, that's better than Melody constantly stealing the blanket at night," Diego complained as we stepped into the room.

"Better keep that to yourself."

Melody and Ava glared at us both.

"See I can already tell they're plotting how to kill us," Diego said, and I shook my head.

"All right, I'll see you later." I slapped hands with him and went to tell Melody good night. Despite her harsh look, she continued to stare at him.

"Melody, good to see you again. I'm heading out."

"What is this I hear about you texting with Sharon?" Melody probed.

"Huh?"

"Melody," Ava hissed.

"Blaze, you're my friend, but if you're cheating, I would

be very disappointed in you." Melody crossed her arms over her chest.

"I'm not texting with Sharon."

"Yes you were!" Ava snapped.

"No I wasn't."

She jumped up in my face and we were like two bulls with our chests heaving up and down, nostrils flared. Diego came over and got in between us.

"What happened that quickly?"

"He's cheating," Ava spat.

The music in the room turned off, and all eyes were on us. All I wanted to do was go to bed and get some food in my stomach.

"I'm not cheating."

"Then who were you texting? Show us," she demanded.

"None of your business."

"You see, all he cares about is money," Ava complained and started to walk away. I blocked her from leaving.

"First off, I didn't cheat. Secondly, I don't have Sharon's number."

"Then who were you texting?" Her eyes scanned my face for any signs of a lie.

"The same person that bought you Peter."

She gasped, and my upper lip lifted in delight.

"Who's Peter?" Joel questioned the room.

"It's—"

Before I could answer, she covered my mouth with her hand.

"Nobody. And this conversation is over." Ava stormed out of the room.

"Come on, Diego, we need to go check on her," Melody said.

"Who's Peter?" Diego interrogated.

"I'll tell you later." Melody gripped him by the arm to get him to shut up.

"Hell, we still don't know who Peter is," Kimberly blurted out.

"Did you steal my wallet?" Joel turned to her.

"What!"

That was my cue to get out before more drama popped up.

Chapter Eight

Blze

wo days later.

The second challenge was happening today, and the bleachers were filling with audience members. Hair and makeup were putting us together. I had an interview before we started filming, and they asked us to wear the white coats with the title of the show across the back. It was corny, but I figured I would play along as smoothly as possible to avoid any problems. Sharon hadn't said a word to me since we stepped on stage, and I was happy about that. Ava seemed to be in a better mood, but she still wasn't talking to me. I didn't know why I cared, but I did. I promised after this challenge I would apologize for bringing up Peter the other night at the party. Makeup finished and stood to the side as the camera crew panned in close, a reporter from Miami Seven News standing next to me.

"Are we ready?" he probed.

"Ready."

"Good. Just a few questions, then you can get started on the challenge."

"Great."

"Again, I'm Jorge, and you'll look directly into that camera."

"Gotcha."

The camera guy counted down from three.

"Hello, Miami Seven, it's me, Jorge Rodriguez, with one of the contestants from *America's Next Top Chemist*. Nice to meet you, Blaze."

"Thanks for having me, Jorge."

"So tell us how the competition is going so far?"

"Everything is going good."

"You won the first challenge, correct?"

"I did."

"What are your thoughts going into this new challenge?"

"Same as I did the first day, focus, and stay on top of the goal."

"Who do you think is your biggest competition?"

I scanned the stage and stared at Ava.

"Blaze."

"Uhm... I don't think of them as my competition."

"What would you do if you won?"

"I'd use the money to reinvest in my company."

"Good luck, Blaze, we're going to be watching. Back to the studio." Jorge signaled to cut the camera and thanked me again.

"Contestants, time to line up!" the production assistant called for us on the stage. I lined up next to Kimberly. Joel was in the middle next to Asher, and Ava was on the end.

"Welcome back, ladies and gentlemen. Are you ready for the second challenge?" Teddi quizzed.

"Yesss!!!"

"I love that you are ready. Let's have our judges come back out. Give them a raise of the hands."

"Yay!!"

"Sharon, you're looking beautiful, and Danny, how are you?"

"Doing good. Happy to be back," Danny answered.

"Contestants, are you ready?"

"Yes!"

"This challenge is individual, all about your knowledge."

The audience started to get riled up. Some called my name, and a few called Joel's name for some reason.

"The way it will work is that each person has a buzzer in front of them. Hit the buzzer if you know the answer."

"Let's go, Ava! Let's go!" the audience screamed.

"We need the audience to quiet down so they can hear the questions," Teddi explained, putting a finger against her mouth. "You'll have a few simple questions, and you'll receive points. But you have 10 seconds to answer when you hit the buzzer." Teddi motioned to the large clock on the wall that was counting down.

"If you can't answer, someone can buzz in to answer and win that point."

"Oohhh!" The crowd clapped their hands.

The lights dimmed on the stage, and my palm hovered over the buzzer.

"Judges, are you ready?"

"We're ready," Danny said.

"Whirl the liquid in the top bottle, it creates a vortex as it drains into the bottom bottle." Teddi hinted.

Buzz!

"Tornado in a bottle," Ava answered.

"Ava! Ava!"

Sharon rolled her eyes, and Teddi motioned to the crowd to calm down.

"One point for Ava. This item deals with density, sugar to a liquid, it causes the solution to become more dense."

"Rainbow in a glass!" Joey yelled.

"Correct. One point for Joel."

I cracked my neck left to right and squared my shoulder.

"The competition is heating up. We have Joel and Ava both with one point. Blaze, Kimberly, and Asher zero."

"Oohhhh."

"After we take a break, things get crazier. Be right back." Teddi signed off.

Production staff ran on stage to reset the lights, makeup scrambled over to touch us up, and I grabbed a bottle of water from the assistant.

"This is going to be an easy win," Joel mentioned.

"It just started. Don't get too happy."

"I'm ready."

"Five minutes!" staff yelled.

"She hasn't moved." Joel tapped me on my shoulder and pointed at Ava.

Her eyes were locked on the screen, hand next to the buzzer.

"Welcome back to *Next Top Chemist*. If you're just joining us, we're on to the second challenge of the game. Contestants have to answer questions by hitting a buzzer."

"Yayyay!!"

"This next one will earn five points. The experiment includes hydrogen peroxide, a jar, fire and...a piece of uncooked pasta."

Buzz!

"Pasta rocket!" I shouted.

"Correct!" Teddi excitedly clapped for me.

Ava tossed her hair behind her ear.

"We have Blaze with five points and Ava and Joel with one point."

"Blaze! Blaze!"

"The next question is a little easier. What year did the Rube challenge begin?"

Buzz!

"Originally in 1949 at Purdue University and held annually until 1956, then revived in 1983," Ava answered quickly.

"Correct!"

Ava jumped up and down excitedly.

"Six points for Ava." Teddi walked over to Ava and held the mic up to her face.

The crowd simmered down.

"How are you feeling so far, Ava?"

"Ready to win," Ava replied.

"You heard her, everybody. Keep it going, This experiment was won in 2007. What was the experiment?"

Buzz!

"The task of juicing an orange into a pitcher and pouring the pitcher into a cup in 20 or more steps," I responded.

"Blaze is coming up on you. Going into the final round we have Ava with six points, Blaze with ten points."

"Yes! Yes!"

"Judges, what do you think so far?"

"I have my money on Ava." Carl pointed at Ava.

"My money is on Ava," Danny said.

"I think Joel has a chance to take it home," Sharon quipped.

Ava held the fakest smile on her face.

"We have one final question that is worth twenty points." Teddi shuffled the cards in her hand.

"Yay!!"

"Okay, focus. The final question is Who is known as the 'father of biochemistry'?"

Buzz!

"Carl Neuberg, the discover of carboxylation," Ava shouted after hitting the buzzer.

"Ava is correct!" Teddi waved at the camera.

Ava started to jump up and down, covering her face with her hands.

"We'll be right back with the elimination round."

"Five minutes!" the stage assistant yelled.

"Everyone line up here," Abigail said, looking through her sheets.

"Good job," Joel told Ava.

"Thanks."

Our eyes connected, and I nodded in recognition of what she'd pulled off.

"America, we have our second elimination tonight. Judges, what do you say?" Teddi questioned.

"After deliberation, we vote for Kimberly," Carl explained. Kimberly waved, and Teddi moved toward her with the microphone.

"Kimberly, this was your second time being here. What do you have to say?"

"I'm just happy to be here and grateful for the opportunity." Kimberly kept her smile on and grinned.

"Once again, we thank you for watching and can't wait to crown the winner. See you next time." Teddi winked her left eye at the camera.

"This is bullshit!" Kimberly cursed and stormed off the stage.

"Sore loser," Joel mumbled.

"Everyone, you have the rest of the evening for yourselves. But be prepared for the final contest," Abigail called over the bullhorn.

Ava went to walk off, and I jogged up to her as security held the doors open.

"Nice catch on the questions."

"Thanks."

The van was open, and we climbed in to sit in the middle seats. Kimberly was cursing and throwing a fit.

"This is a Setup. My machine is not working," Kimberly complained.

"Kimberly, all of the machines were tested," Abigail told her.

"I don't agree. You're just taking up for your favorites." Kimberly pointed to the back seat at Ava and me.

"Favorites!" Ava blurted out.

"Don't act like you're not being set up to win. You or your boyfriend."

"We're not together," we both answered at the same time.

"Kimberly, we've given you multiple chances to play. Sorry you just didn't get this one." Abigail shut the door and sat up front.

"Bitch," Kimberly mumbled under her breath.

The van pulled off and headed back to the hotel. It was coming down to me, Ava, and Joel for the most part. Asher wouldn't last long. He didn't come across as being excited by the audience and connecting with them. Fifteen minutes later, we arrived at the hotel. The door opened, and I watched Kimberly jump out. Ava got out next, and a few girls ran up to her.

"Ava! Ava! Can we have an autograph?" they yelled.

"Uhm..."

"Blaze! OMG! Can we get a picture?"

"Sure, I'll let you have your autograph first." I stepped to the side so Ava could sign the pictures.

"Please, Ava!"

"Of course. Who should I make it out to?" Ava questioned.

"Me, my name is Tammy, we're into science like you." The fifteen-year-old girls screamed in excitement, and I smiled as she wrote her name on the picture.

"I love to see girls in science and STEM. Keep up the good work." Ava handed the pictures back.

"Turning into a celebrity," I muttered in her ear.

She elbowed me in the stomach.

"Shut up."

"Thanks, ladies." I smiled in the photo, and they hugged me.

* * *

Ava hit the elevator button. I let her walk ahead of me, with Joel and Asher coming behind me. Her perfume lingered in the air as I stepped up beside her, and our arms grazed each other.

"Good game, Ava," Asher complimented her.

"Thanks, Asher."

"He talks," Joel joked.

The elevator burst into laughter at his comment.

"What was with Kimberly?" Ava asked.

"Seriously, she's crazy. After you guys left the party, she was trying to sleep with me," Asher brought up.

"She's kind of cute," Joel replied.

All eyes turned toward him.

"What?"

Ding!

"Thank God." Ava stepped off and moved toward her suite door. The doors closed again and went up to the next floor, and I started to get off.

"Drinks later!" Joel yelled out through the elevator, but I blew him off.

I slid the key in the door and walked in and tossed it on the table. Kicking off my shoes, I lay down on the couch and ran a hand across my face. My eyes were getting heavy, and I felt my body relax as the day started to cool down.

Chapter Nine

Ava

Later that night.

The wine glass was filled, and I waited for Melody to give her toast as we sat at the to celebrate my win tonight.

"Ava, I'm so proud of you! I can't wait for the final competition."

"Thank you so much. I'm so close."

"You are, and I can see it now with your name in lights." Melody raised her hands in the air and shifted in her seat.

"How many drinks have you had?" I giggled at her expression.

"This is my second one."

"Don't let her fool you, Ava," Diego barked as he drank his cognac.

Melody poked her lips out for a kiss. Diego groaned and kissed her on the lips. She wiped the lipstick from his lips.

"Where's Blaze?" Melody questioned.

"Right here." He pulled the chair out and sat down next to me as Diego poured him a glass of cognac.

"Thanks, D," Blaze said.

"What took you so long?" Melody asked. The waitress brought out our plates of food.

"Thank you," I said, picking up my fork.

"I didn't know when you would come, so I didn't order you anything." Melody picked up her spoon and ate her autumn spice mixed with wild rice.

I ordered falafel with steamed veggies on the side.

"I'll have what she has." He pointed at my plate.

"Copycat." I cleared my throat.

He took a sip of the drink.

"I'll have that right out for you, sir," the waitress said.

"Thank you," Blaze replied.

"What do you think is the last challenge?" Melody asked and ate a piece of Diego's chicken.

"Has to be an experiment."

"That Kimberly girl was crazy. Did you see how she stormed off?"

"You should have seen her in the van."

"Blaze, you did good too." Melody popped a piece of bread in her mouth.

He chuckled, leaning his elbows on the table. "Today is all about Ava."

I looked at him suspiciously. He'd given me a compliment; more than likely something was up that he wanted.

"Did you happen to fall or have a cold?" I felt the top of his head.

"What? Why do you say that?"

"Because you're being nice to me."

"The competition is even now, and you did a good job."

"But you're going to lose."

"That's what you think?"

"It's what I know. We're riding the wave to the top." I slapped hands with Melody.

"Have to agree with Ava. CrimsonBio is going to take the bag home."

"Newton Industries is not too far behind, being the man of the company."

"Oh my God! Here he goes." I groaned.

"CrimsonBio is a great lab, but we are on the cusp of doing research that can take things even further," Blaze argued.

I took a bite of the falafel and rice, and the waitress brought his food and laid it on the table.

"Thanks."

"That may be true, but we have characters in CrimsonBio."

"When I win, just remember my character in Jamaica."

I'd forgotten about the Jamaica bet.

"You're not missing much," I murmured.

"She's scared," Blaze joked.

"What makes you think I'm scared?"

"Diego can see from here you're terrified I'll win," Blaze taunted, sipping his drink.

"My girl is going to win, just be prepared to eat crow."

Melody and I high-fived.

"Let him know, best friend," I egged her on.

"What are you getting for dessert?"

"Probably a brownie."

"Did you tell her about the dress for the wedding?" Melody investigated.

"When did you know about this wedding?" I probed, turning in my chair to face him.

"When you and Melody went shopping the other day," Blaze answered.

"We're going, Ava. It'll be fun, besides I don't like most of Blaze's family." Melody rolled her eyes.

"She's had enough." Diego took the drink out of her hands, and I giggled.

"That's cool, Melody. I feel the same way."

The tall, blonde, slim waitress approached our table.

"Would you like any desserts or anything else?"

"No, I'll take the check."

"You're leaving!" Melody shrieked.

"I need to get some sleep and get up early for the competition." I placed the napkin on the table.

"The check would be great," Diego said, passing Melody a glass of water.

"Fine, guess I will leave too," Melody grunted.

"Remember I might need your help tomorrow," I reminded her.

"Can I get a to-go box?" Blaze asked.

"Yes, sir."

"I'll take a piece of the cheesecake to go," Melody called out, and Diego groaned.

I chuckled at those two, loving the way he treated her, supportive in everything.

"All right, time for this one to get to bed." Diego helped her out of the chair.

"Give me a hug." Melody reached over and gave me a hug.

"Get her to bed, Diego. I'll see you in the morning."

"You need us to walk you to your room?" Diego questioned.

I waved him off. "I'm a big girl. I'll be fine."

"Blaze can walk you to your room."

Blaze looked surprised.

"He doesn't need to walk me to my room."

Sharon appeared at our table, and I put on a fake smile.

"Well, don't tell me the happy couple is in different

rooms." Sharon's eyes narrowed at me. Blaze and I peered at each other.

"Sharon, right?" I taunted, pointed my finger at her.

"You know that's my name," she spat.

"Sorry, forgive me, the wine went to my head."

"I never knew Blaze to be into a woman that drinks so much," Sharon snipped.

I grabbed Blaze's hand, and he looked down at me.

"Ava can drink as much as she wants since I'm here." He smiled.

"Miss Langford, your card declined." The hostess approached her and held out her card.

"You must be mistaken."

"I ran it twice," the hostess replied.

"Run it again," Sharon snapped.

I held a hand over my mouth to avoid laughing.

"Baby, let's go. I think you need to get off your feet," Blaze told me, and those words out of his mouth threw me off.

"Su...sure," I stuttered.

"Have a nice evening, Sharon," Melody teased, and I giggled behind her as we headed to the elevator, holding hands.

"Ohh, that girl is so sprung on you." I followed him into the elevator.

"She's more than sprung. Obsessed," Melody quipped.

"I don't know what her problem is with me."

"From what I see, the chemistry is on a high level."

"What are you talking about, Melody?"

"I mean you two haven't stopped holding hands since we've been on the elevator," Melody remarked, and our eyes went down to our hands. I snatched mine away and hit the button for my floor.

"Whatever, Melody."

She laughed, and the elevator stopped on their floor.

"Don't do anything I wouldn't do," Melody teased, waving at me.

"Diego, please put her to sleep." I sighed dramatically.

He smirked and wrapped an arm around her shoulders.

"Take care of her, bro." Diego pointed at me.

"Good night, Diego."

The doors closed, and I took a step forward to prepare to get off the elevator.

"Sharon's harmless," he mumbled.

I turned my head and nodded.

"She's funny."

"What do you mean?"

"It must really be good if she's still trying to get you." The doors opened, and I stepped off and sauntered to my door.

"Good night, Ava!" he called out.

"Night."

"Wait!" he barked and jogged to my door. I pushed it open, strolled in, and turned the light on.

"What?"

"No matter what happens tomorrow, I want you to know you're not half bad." Blaze nudged me in the arm.

"I guess that's a compliment."

"Do you know what you're going to do?" he investigated.

* * *

His cologne was enticing, and I didn't know if he was being genuine or trying to find out my plans for the final competition. I shut the door behind him and stared into his eyes, poking out my lip.

"What's your angle?"

"Ava."

"Come on, tell me what you want. You'll probably take my secrets to Sharon!"

I pointed at the door.

"Are you serious?"

"Yep. I find it interesting you're asking about my final competition."

He shrugged.

"I was just being friendly. Sorry." He turned to leave, and I reached over and grabbed his arm. He looked down at my hand.

"Were you texting her the other night?" I needed to know.

Blaze's eyes ran from my arm up to my face and back to my lips, and I removed my hand from his arm.

"You're jealous."

"No I'm not." I blew a breath.

"Yes you are."

"Please stop trying to make this about me liking you."

"You like me." He smiled.

"Oh gosh, you're an ass."

I stomped over to the fridge, opened the door, and grabbed a Coke. I popped it open, and it spilled all over my clothes.

"Shit!" I put it down on the counter and grabbed a napkin to clean myself up.

"That wasn't Sharon, it was another person."

He passed another napkin to me.

"Of course it was." I scoffed.

"Sharon's not the only one that might be obsessed."

My face scrunched up. "Having many women you're sleeping around with doesn't matter to me."

"What matters to you then?" He closed the space between us.

I looked up into his eyes. "Winning," I said forcefully.

He moved a piece of my hair out of my face.

"What are you—"

"Do you want to kiss me, Ava?"

My mouth dropped agape. "Yes," I whispered, dropping my hands beside me.

"I'm not your enemy."

"Shut up and kiss me."

I cupped both sides of his face, leaned against his chest, and pressed my lips to his mouth. He brushed his lips across my bottom lip, gripping both sides of my waist.

"Mmmmm..."

Ring!

I pushed back out of his hold and reached for my phone in my pocket.

"Hel...llo." I ran a hand through my hair and walked away from him.

"Why do you sound weird?" Trisha questioned.

I went to sit down on the couch.

"Uhmm... I'm not weird, just tired."

"Something is going on, and you're lying."

"I'll let you handle your phone call," Blaze told me, and I tried to cover the phone before Trisha could hear him.

"Who is that?" she asked.

"Nobody."

I watched him leave my room, and I stood up to lock the door and stared at his back as he went to the elevator. I fell back on the couch and groaned.

"Let me guess. Blaze was there."

"Trisha."

"Nothing wrong with having a little conversation, maybe a little kiss."

"A lot wrong with that."

"Ava, it's a reality show."

"Yeah, it's worth five hundred thousand dollars."

"He's cute and smart, plus has money."

"I don't care."

"Was the sex good?"

"We didn't sleep together, we just kissed." I removed my jacket, stood up, and walked to the bedroom. I grabbed my night clothes and hair wrap.

"I mean, it's only a matter of time before you fall into bed together."

"I can't."

"Why not?"

I put the call on speaker and pinned my hair up in a ponytail and hair wrap.

"He's my one—"

"Girl, if you tell me he's your enemy one more time, like you're Batman and he's the Joker—"

I laughed at her comment. "Shut up, Trisha."

"I'm serious. Just have fun."

"I will after I win the competition."

"You're killing me."

"Oh, shut up."

"Does he kiss well?"

I stepped over to the shower and turned it on, checking the temperature.

"It was all right," I lied, still feeling the remnants of his lips on my tongue.

"I hear the shower, so you must be getting ready for bed."

"Yep, tomorrow's the last day."

"Sending you all positive vibes and call me soon as you win."

"Thanks, Trisha, talk tomorrow." We ended the call, and I removed my pants, bra, and underwear and stepped into the shower to wash off my makeup and think of how the next day would go. I grabbed the towel and soap and went to wash my neck. I closed my eyes and moved it down to my left breast, then right, and I moaned subconsciously.

"Blaze," I moaned, my eyes popping open in surprise.

I needed to get out of Miami.

Chapter Ten

Ava

"Audience, give it up for the final contestants!" Teddi screamed.

"Yay!!!"

"We have Ava playing for CrimsonBio, Blaze for Newton Industries, Joel with Ankerson Labs, and finally Asher for BioChrome labs."

Screams and cheers erupted in the audience.

"Our judges are here and ready to crown the winner."

Danny and Carl waved to the crowd, and Sharon stood up and picked up the microphone.

"For my background, this show has done wonders for supporting women scientists. Even Ava getting this far is exciting." Sharon put the mic down, waved, and sat down in her chair, narrowing her eyes at me.

"For this final competition, you're doing an experiment you've chosen, but we have a surprise."

"Oh. Shit." Joel wiped his hands on his pants.

"That's right. On top of your experiment, we have chosen one for you to complete, and you'll need to grab the ingredients."

"You can back out now if you want," Blaze whispered in my ear.

I grinned and waved to the audience. "Not on your life," I muttered, looking forward.

"The first two people to hit the buzzer will see the judges, and a winner will be crowned." Teddi pointed for us to move to our individual stations, the music got cut off, and the lights went down.

"Ava, what experiment are you doing today?" Teddi asked.

"Copper and nitric acid."

The audience clapped their hands.

"Joel, what about you?"

"Teddi, I'm going to be doing the thermite reaction," Joel explained.

"Seems like we have a real challenge here. Okay, the audience has chosen the second challenge. Contestants, are you ready?"

"Yes!" all four of us yelled.

"The audience has chosen *coloring fire*!" Teddi pulled the card out and faced the audience.

The sign for the audience to react with applause came on.

Clapping!

"Remember you have two experiments. We'll be right back, America." Teddi cut to break.

"Everybody, your ingredients are behind you and in front of you." Abigail motioned for the cabinet holding all of the test tubes and equipment.

"Your buzzer is ready, and we have the fire department on standby. Any questions?" Abigail asked.

"No," everyone answered at the same time.

"Great. As soon as we come back, the clock will start," Abigail said.

Makeup applied more lipstick and the hair stylist brushed out my long hair. I'd decided for the final competition to wear my hair straight.

"Five minutes!"

I cracked my knuckles, rolled my shoulders, closed my eyes, and said a little prayer.

"Please let me win, God."

"Showtime!" staff called out.

"Tonight is the final night of the challenge. We are going to crown a winner. Are you ready to see who wins!" Teddi shouted, cupped her ear to hear the audience.

"Ava! Ava!" the audience screamed, and I felt the love.

"All right, set the clock. On your mark. Go!"

I grabbed the basket in front of me and ran to the cabinet to grab everything I needed for the coloring experiment. I tapped my fingers against the basket, thinking of the amount to disburse and have time. Joel ran back and forth, picking out items, and I noticed Asher starting to work on the first experiment without grabbing for the second one.

"Shit!" I sped up and decided on making blue, remembering to use copper chloride. I picked up everything and ran back to my station, placing my goggles and gloves on. I worked on the first experiment, separating the different ingredients, grabbed the test tube, and poured hydrochloric acid.

"What are you doing now, Ava?" Teddi and the camera man stood in front of my station. I smiled and motioned to the first tube.

"I have everything separated with water and copper chips."

"How are you feeling about this so far?"

"I feel pretty good."

"You have some stiff competition. Good luck."

They went over to Asher, and he held up the sugar he was using in a container.

"Asher, you came in last so what are your thoughts?"

"I think I'm the underdog and you can't count me out." Asher pushed the goggles back on.

"Good luck, guys."

"Shit!" I heard Joel curse and looked up to see him move the tray out of the way and run to grab more items. Blaze was talking with Teddi now, and I wished I was a fly on the wall to hear what he was saying. Did he have a dream about me after the kiss, or was it just a momentary thing?

I shook my head.

"Not the time," I told myself.

I poured the ingredients together and stood back as they came together, then moved to the coloring fire and set up the Copper(I) chloride.

Buzz!

"Done!" Blaze shouted, and the room erupted in screams.

I wiped my brow and focused on moving between both stations. Noticing the flames coming up, I grinned. I turned to the nitric acid experiment, and my mouth dropped open in happiness.

"I'm finished."

I jumped up in excitement.

"Hit the buzzer!" I heard someone shout.

Buzz!

"Done!" I jumped up and down in excitement, Joel tossed his glove on the floor, and Asher gave me a hug.

"We have our two final contestants. Joel and Asher, you both were great, but we have to say goodbye for now."

Everybody gave them a round of applause, and Joel gave me a hug.

"You're not so bad after all," Joel said.

"Thanks, Joel—I think." I giggled.

"Ava and Blaze, you can step forward in front of the judges. We'll be right back," Teddi said.

The audience clapped, and I calmed my nerves and waited for the final decision.

"You did good," Blaze spoke.

"Thanks."

"No matter what happens, I'm glad it's you next to me." He smiled.

"Me too." I blushed and smiled back at him.

"We're back with our final two contestants. One of them will go home with five hundred thousand dollars and be the official winner of *America's Next Top Chemist.*"

Clap!

"Ava and Blaze, are you ready to face the judges?" Teddi asked.

"Yes."

"Judges, you've been watching the entire time. What are your thoughts?"

"I think for style and technique, Blaze would be my pick." Sharon hit the buzzer, and Blaze's name came up on the screen.

"Danny, what do you have to say?" Teddi asked.

Danny held his hands in front of him and watched us both.

"Throughout the competition, Blaze has really shown the grit, technique, and willingness to take a chance," Danny said.

My heart and stomach started to drop.

"Is that your final answer?"

Danny hit the buzzer and Blaze's name popped up.

I couldn't show defeat, so I stood up tall and watched as my dreams were going down the drain.

"Carl, you're the final vote. Who did you pick?"

"We didn't agree on much through the challenges, but we have to give it to Blaze, he knocked it outta the park with the barking dog experiment." Carl hit the buzzer on his desk, and the confetti dropped down and the crowd went crazy and stood up.

"Blaze Newton, you are the winner of *America's Next Top Chemist*! How do you feel?" Teddi pulled him up front, and I removed my hand to cower in the corner and give him space. Before I could turn away, he gripped my elbow and pulled me up front with him.

"What are you doing?" I whispered.

"Just stand here," Blaze replied.

"Blaze! Blaze!" the audience yelled.

"Thank you, Teddi, and the judges for this opportunity, and especially the audience for keeping me motivated. But most of all I want to thank my fellow contestants." Blaze raised our hands together up in the air. I waved and thanked everyone.

"I couldn't have done this game if Ava wasn't a tough opponent, so I'd love it if she accepted half of the money," Blaze explained, and my eyes went wide in shock. Tears started to pool in my eyes, and I reached up, not thinking of where we were, and kissed him on the lips.

"Ahhhh!" the audience moaned, and I pulled back quickly, remembering I was on national TV.

"Sorry!"

"There you have it, America. We not only picked a winner, but possibly a love connection," Teddi teased. I couldn't say anything back and continued to cry when I saw Melody run up on stage.

"Ava! Oh my God!" Melody screamed, hugging Blaze.

Diego shook his hand and reached to give me a hug.

"Thank you, Blaze, but are you sure?" I probed, not wanting to hear this was just for show.

"I'm positive. You deserve it just as much as me," he answered.

"What about the bet?"

"I thought you weren't interested in the bet." Blaze's right brow hiked.

"I'm not. I just wanted to make sure the money didn't come with anything."

"Like what? The kiss?"

"What kiss?" Melody asked.

"Melody...shush."

"How about we go celebrate? We haven't hit up any clubs," Diego proposed.

"That'll be great. Come on, Ava." Melody grabbed my hand.

"Okay, but we have to be at work the day after tomorrow."

She waved me off. "I'm the boss, I'll write you a note." She laughed, and Abigail stopped us to do interviews.

"Ava, this is Jorge from Miami Seven News," Abigail introduced us.

"Congratulations, Blaze, how are you feeling?" Jorge probed.

"I feel good and ready to get to work."

"The money you've decided to split with Ava. Why is that?"

"Because I know she works hard, and I personally know the work that CrimsonBio lab is doing will help change lives," Blaze explained, and my heart started to beat faster at the man standing before me. The jerk that constantly made my blood pressure rise was not all that bad.

"Ava, you came in second, but still going home with a prize. What does that mean?"

"It means that not only will I be able to benefit CrimsonBio, but a local center."

"You're competing for a local center back home?"

"I was, and I'm happy to bring anything back that I can."

"Glad you're doing something amazing."

"Thank you."

"Singing off, back to you at Miami Seven News."

Abigail handed some paperwork to Blaze, and I went to follow Melody out of the building.

"Where's Blaze?"

"He's talking with Abigail," I said.

"Going to celebrate. You guys will end up being the 'it' couple." Melody slid in the rental car, and Diego shut the door. I jumped in the backseat, grabbed the seatbelt, and watched Sharon run behind Blaze as he came out of the building.

"She looks more and more desperate," Melody called out, and I agreed.

"Exactly, and you'd think when he kissed me, she would get the hint."

Two pairs of eyes looked back at me.

"What?"

"You kissed him on live TV."

"No I didn't," I chortled.

"Uhm, yes you did, Ava." Melody pulled up her phone and scrolled to the video footage and played the last few seconds.

"I want to share this with Ava," Blaze repeated, and I jumped in his arms and kissed him on the lips.

"I think I'm going to be sick."

"Don't throw up in this car!" Diego shouted.

"Why did you let me do that?" I yelled at Melody.

"I didn't know you'd jump in his arms."

"You're supposed to know these things about me as my best friend."

"It'll go away in a day or two."

The passenger door opened and Blaze slid over, passing me an envelope.

"What's this?"

I turned it around.

"Your half."

"Wait! You were serious?"

"Yeah, what do you think? I go around giving people that much money for fun?"

"Thank you. Seriously."

"Are you going to Jamaica?"

"I can't, sorry. I have too much work to do," I lied, and out the corner of my eye, Melody shook her head.

"No worries."

"That's it? You won't beat me down about the bet?"

"No, I'll find someone else," he said, and my eyes narrowed to slits.

"Plenty of women you can hang out with. Your cousin won't mind," Diego called out, and Melody hit him on the arm.

"Good, it's settled. Thank you again."

"You're welcome." Blaze's eyes held contact.

"We're going back to the hotel, change, and then club," Melody explained.

I put the check in my pocket and looked out of the

window, watching as the audience stood outside waiting for autographs. I waved back but didn't stop to get out. Being that important wasn't on my agenda for the reasons why I came out here.

* * *

Later that night.

Life in Miami was insane, and I couldn't believe the atmosphere was non-stop, wall to wall women dancing and men in VIP areas that watched. The music was everything you'd expect from the late R&B, rave type of music. Melody had forced me to let loose tonight, and I wore a short, silver one-shoulder glitter dress. It showed my body curves, and the little butt that poked out that was the perfect size to fit in a guy's hand. I kept my hair long and applied red lipstick and eyelashes that I accidentally almost glued shut.

"Show these folks how LA women get down, Ava!" Melody screamed, and I moved my hips and twisted around and popped my booty.

"You did amazing today, friend."

"Thank you."

"I can't wait to bring in more staff."

"No work talk tonight. All about having fun." I grabbed her hand, made her turn and dip, and came back up.

A few bottle girls walked through the crowd with champagne bottles and sparklers on top, with the latest Megan Thee Stallion bumping. When the girls get together, we form a line and start dancing together. I threw my hands in the air when the DJ mixed the song and went to Old-school Foxy Brown.

"Here, take a shot!" Melody passed me a drink.

I grabbed it out of her hand.

"We are toasting to the future as businesswomen and CrimsonBio!" Melody yelled, clinking glasses and tossing back her drink. I gulped mine down, pursed my lips, and popped my tongue to get the taste down.

"Woo, lord, that was strong."

"You want to try the hookah bar?" Melody pointed at the section next to us that was smoking.

"No, I'm fine, let's go dance with the crowd."

We linked hands, and she motioned to Diego that we were going farther into the crowd.

"Stay where I can see you!" Diego yelled out, and Melody smacked her lips.

"He's so overprotective."

"He's being a husband. Relax and let him do his job," I shouted in her ear as we pushed through the crowd to get closer to the DJ.

"Would you say the same thing if someone was acting like that with you?"

"Yeah, you know how many crazy folks are out here."

I snapped my fingers, shook my shoulders, dipped low, and popped left to right.

"Ladies, if you're feeling sexy tonight, let me hear you scream!" the DJ shouted.

"Yess!!" I yelled back.

The effects of the shot were taking over me, and I couldn't wait to find someone to make out with before I went back home to LA.

"He's cute." I pointed at the guy that was standing on the wall next to the DJ booth.

"Who?"

"Ladies shot!" A bottle girl came around.

"No, I'm fine."

"One more, Ava. We're grown and having fun." Melody picked the shot glasses off the tray and passed it to me.

"The last one."

"Tell me, which guy did you see?"

"He has the black sweater on, blue jeans, on the wall right there." I motioned to the sexy dark skin and long dreads talking with his friends.

"He's cute, but he doesn't look like your type."

"Shit!" I dropped the alcohol on my dress when someone bumped into me from behind.

"Can you say excuse me? You bumped into my friend," Melody demanded.

"It's okay, Melody." I tried to pull her away, but she got in the guy's face.

"She shouldn't have been drinking on the main floor," he barked back.

"We can drink wherever we want. I don't see a sign." Melody pointed to his chest.

"Just ignore her." I tried to calm the situation down.

"Lady, if you don't get your drunk ass away from me—" He stepped in her face.

"Or what?" Melody grabbed a bottle of champagne from a bottle girl that walked by and poured it on top of his head.

I covered my mouth as my eyes scanned for Diego, but I didn't see him.

"Bitch!" He reached to grab Melody, and I pushed him back but didn't move him one inch.

"That's not happening, man. You can step back." Blaze jumped in between the guy and us.

"Who the fuck are you?" he argued.

"The man that won't stand by and let you hit a woman."

"Blaze, let me at him!" Melody yelled, and I grabbed her by the arm, moving her behind me.

"Fuck you and her." He reared back and swung, but Blaze ducked low, came back up and clenched his fist, hitting him with a left hook.

"Oohhh!" The crowd and the music stopped as the guy tried to come back at Blaze and security came around to break it up.

"Y'all have to go!" security said.

"What? We didn't do anything," I shouted.

"That's the one that poured a bottle on my boyfriend," a girl wearing a terrible blonde wig, shorts, and a tube top fussed, popping her gum.

"He bumped into me first," I defended myself.

"Put her out!"

"Make me," I spat.

"Bitch!" She reached for my hair, and Melody charged at her, but her friend came out of nowhere and jumped on Melody's back. The entire night had gone bad, and I was fighting and trying to keep Melody in my line of sight while Blaze was being removed from the club.

* * *

Clack!

The police officer shut the jail door, and I scooted over as another group of women were let in the holding cell. The place smelled of piss, rotten fish, and onions, the floor was dirty, and the walls had graffiti scrawled across them.

"I feel like I'm going crazy," Melody mumbled to herself.

"This is all your fault," I muttered, crossing my legs.

"Stop yelling," Melody fussed.

"Aye! You two little bitches, shut up."

A woman with tattoos across both arms, a leather vest, and an eye patch marched over to us. "Bet you're not from around here." She reached out to touch my hair, but I moved my head.

"We're not, and she's not in her right mind," I tried to plead Melody's case.

"I thought so, because everybody knows Big Amy." She pointed at herself.

"Big Amy, or whoever you are, I don't need to shut up," Melody spat.

Big Amy chuckled, and the entire room laughed.

"She must think this *Orange is the New Black* shit." Big Amy spit the toothpaste out of her mouth and stared into Melody's eyes.

"Big Amy, sit down! You two, let's go." A police officer pointed at me and Melody. I released a shallow breath and jumped up to pull her away from another situation. The gate opened, the guard escorted us out, and I saw Blaze.

"I'll see you around, little momma!" Big Amy yelled out.

Chapter Eleven

Blaze

The same night.

Diego stood with an angry glare on his face as I pushed open the door of the police station, and Melody, Ava, and I walked out. I wasn't expecting our night to end up like this with me defending Ava and getting arrested for public disturbance when we were in the right.

"Diego."

"Are you hurt?"

"No."

"Did they touch you?"

"No."

"Then don't talk to me until we get home," he spat as he drove off. It was going on two a.m. and he told me he'd talked to Abigail and the network had pulled strings to get us out.

"But—"

"Melody," Ava groaned, rubbing her temple and leaning her head against my shoulder. I was surprised she was being cool about being this close to me after earlier today with Sharon.

109

"Sorry." Melody stared out of the window, and I glanced down to see Diego reach for her hand, and she mouthed *Sorry*.

"When is our flight?" Ava questioned.

"Tomorrow at eleven," Melody replied.

"I just want a shower and bed," Ava muttered.

Five minutes later, we arrived at the hotel. The valet took the keys and Diego helped Melody out as I held the door open for Ava. I said goodnight to Diego and Melody, and turned to Ava, who was standing in the corner with her eyes closed.

"You're not bad with a left punch," I teased, and she grinned.

The bell chimed for her floor.

"Thanks, I appreciate your help." Ava got off the elevator and held her hand in the door to keep it from closing.

"I would do it for anyone."

"I know, and that makes me not think of you as my enemy as much." She held up her thumb and index finger as the level of annoyance she held for me.

I chuckled and clapped my hands.

"I guess I should say thank you."

"Are you going straight to bed?"

My right brow perked up at the question.

"Not really, still wired from tonight."

"I could use some company."

* * *

Our mouths clashed together as the water dripped down her hair. As soon as we'd stepped in her room, we'd decided to shower the day away. Having to deal with a jail cell wasn't the way I wanted to end my trip in Miami. Slowly, I sucked on her neck, rubbing up and down her back as I reached for the towel and soap and told her to turn around.

"I needed this," she groaned as I rubbed across her butt cheeks. I dropped to my knees and spread her legs and slowly circled my tongue around her beautiful pink pussy.

"Blaze!" Ava moaned. I grabbed her left thigh to keep her from falling.

While I moved the towel along her leg, I licked, bit, and kissed along the tiger stripes on her upper hips as I further explored her sex. The moment she grabbed the back of my head, I sucked even deeper and pushed my finger back and forth, causing her to rock. She almost fell over, which was my cue to stop. After I kissed back up along her neck, I pulled her hair to the side and sucked on her ear, pushing my hard, thick shaft firmly against her ass.

"I need to be inside of you now."

She nodded.

"Turn the water off, and we'll take it to the bedroom."

Ava turned and reached down to grip my dick, stroking up and down.

"Shit! Ava." I sucked on her neck, lifted her leg, and tapped the tip of my dick against her entrance.

"Mmmmm…"

I reached behind her and turned off the water and grabbed a towel to wrap around her, then I picked up the next towel to clean her off. She led me to her bedroom, and I reached down to remove a condom from my pants and tossed it on the bed.

"You won't be needing Peter tonight." I sat down on the bed and extended a hand for her to climb on top.

"That's to be determined," she challenged as she reached for the condom and tore it open with her teeth. She straddled my lap, squeezed my dick, and ran her finger over the precum, bending over to take my bottom lip in her mouth. I grunted, gripped her waist, smacked her on the ass, and lifted her left leg and she eased on top of my member.

"Blaze! Ohh, damn."

I rolled my hips and pinched her nipple, bringing it to my mouth and pumping slowly, to get a rhythm and French kiss between both breasts. Her head fell back, mouth open. Her sex face was something I'd dreamed about many nights while we shared a room together. Ava bit her bottom lip, dropped her right hand on the bed, lay back, and pushed her chest forward.

"Arghhh...Yes!"

The smacking of our skin and the water from her hair dripping onto the bed made the atmosphere grow intense. Was this another challenge? Did she think she would make me come first? I grinned, running my palm up her chest, and gripped her neck, bringing her lips to mine.

"Who's making you feel like this?"

"You are."

"Say my name."

I flipped us over and laid her on her back, picking up my strokes, I held her legs in my arms, lifted her with all my strength, and fucked her standing up. She squeezed around my dick, and I felt her nectar flow like a river as her eyes rolled back in her head.

"Blaze, I'm coming!" she screamed.

"That's right, come for me."

"Ughhh!"

"Fuck! Yes..." I grunted and stroked two more times

until her body trembled in my arms. I gently laid her back down on the bed, pulled out, and lay next to her, catching my breath. She grabbed the comforter and rolled it over on top of us, and we fell asleep with her in my arms.

* * *

The sun beamed down on me, and I groaned, feeling a crick in my neck. I turned to my side and remembered that Ava and I had slept together. I reached over and hugged her from behind, kissing her on the shoulder.

"Morning."

She groaned, turned in my arms, and smiled.

"Morning."

"How do you feel?" I rubbed her leg.

"Fine, what time is it?" Ava looked behind her at the clock.

"Nine-thirty."

"Shit! We have to get dressed." Ava threw the covers off and jumped out of bed.

I slid up on the headboard.

"What time is your flight?" she asked.

"Noon."

We lived in different cities, and I didn't have any type of expectations. This was something serious, but last night we went for two more rounds and showered again after our little nap. If she wanted to see me again, I'd put it in her corner to take the next step. Ava ran into the bathroom with her pants in her hand, no bra, and picked up the toothbrush. I chuckled and got out of bed and picked up my pants and shirt.

"What's funny?" she murmured through the toothpaste.

"Nothing. I'm going to get out of here and pack for my flight." I walked over to her and kissed her on the forehead. Ava spit in the sink and rinsed her mouth out, coming out of the bathroom as I tied my shoes and she slipped her shirt on.

"Last night—"

I peered up at as she hovered over me.

"Yeah, last night."

She sat on the bed, clasping her hands together.

"It was nice."

"Thanks, I guess." I went to jump up and leave.

"Wait! It was more than nice, Blaze, and I didn't expect it to happen."

"I didn't either."

"We live in different states; it wouldn't work."

"I agree."

"You do? I mean, you have enough on your plate."

She lowered her eyes, and I lifted her chin.

"No pressure, Ava. I wasn't expecting this either."

"Friends?" she asked.

The things we did last night wouldn't suggest friends, but I'd let her define whatever she believed so it wasn't awkward.

"Most of the time my one-night stands—"

I raised my hand to stop her from speaking further. Especially anything to do with another man touching her and feeling what I felt last night.

"We're good. Tell Melody and Diego I said I'll call when I make it home."

I walked out of her room, checking my pockets for my key and wallet, and ran into the last person I wanted to see.

"Blaze, what are you still doing here?" Sharon questioned.

The door opened behind me, and Ava held my phone in her hand.

"You forgot this," she said.

Sharon's hands clenched at her side, her jaw tightened, and she turned and stalked off down the hall.

"Thanks."

"Is she all right?"

I shrugged and hit the button of the elevator.

"Who knows?"

* * *

Three days later, I was back home in Boston. I'd taken the first day to sleep. The second day, I'd caught up with family and friends and handled a few emails from work and the network wanting to film the reunion in a few weeks. It was Thursday, the day before the weekend, and I planned on hanging with my boys on Saturday for a game of ball. I sat at my desk, looking over the report from my team, scanning through the numbers they projected to hit once the funding was set. I'd deposited the money from the game show, and after taxes still came home with a good chunk. I sipped on my coffee and made a few notes on some things they could change.

Knock! Knock!

"Come in, Broderick."

"Finally came to work?" Broderick was one of my best friends next to Diego, and he worked as the attorney for the lab.

I slapped hands with him and tossed the report on my desk.

"I'm the boss. I make my own schedule."

"How was Miami?"

"Great."

"You won, bro. I heard you were more than great."

"It was Miami."

"I heard you got arrested."

"Who told you that?"

"Diego." He sat down in the chair, unbuttoning his jacket.

"It was a misunderstanding."

"Something about you protecting your woman," he joked.

I grumbled and leaned back in my chair.

"Man, shut up, fool."

"So it's true?"

"It was Melody and Ava."

"Who's Ava?"

"The girl I told you about I saw at a few conferences."

"The one you labeled your arch rival."

"Something like that."

"Did you get her number?"

"What?"

He shrugged. "I mean, you went to jail over the girl. You must like her."

"She's cool, but we live in two different states."

"You didn't give a valid reason."

"I'm not the relationship type."

"Have you talked to Kenya?"

"Nobody's thinking about her."

"She can help pass the time until your true love comes," he justified it, and I threw my pen at him.

"What do you think of these research proposals?"

"Depending on your timetable, I think you can make them work."

"I want to open another lab."

"Where are you thinking?"

"Not sure yet."

"Have the accountant send me the numbers."

"For sure."

Ring!

I groaned, removed my phone out my pocket, and saw Kenya texting again.

Kenya: Hey are you back in town.

"This girl."

"Who?"

"Kenya." I texted her back.

Me: I'm busy Kenya.

Kenya: I want to go to dinner and talk.

"What does she want?"

"Dinner."

"I thought you two were just sex."

"We are, and she's trying to make it into more."

"Let me guess. Ava is making that a little difficult."

"Ava is just a friend."

"Well, tell your friend I'm single." He rose from his seat, and I growled at him.

"She's not available."

"Are you sure about that?"

Kenya: Hello Blaze?

I looked down at my phone.

Me: Sorry, I'm at work.

"Work on the numbers and worry less about Ava."

"Sounds a little jealous."

"Fuck off." I flipped him off and he cackled and grabbed the report off my desk.

"What are you doing for lunch?" I questioned.

"Probably the burger joint around the corner."

"I might as well join you."

"That's cool."

Ring!

My eyebrows scrunched in annoyance.

"She's calling on FaceTime."

"Block her."

"I don't know."

"You already know you don't see a future with her. Why waste time?"

That made sense, so I declined the call and put the phone back in my pocket.

"I'll meet you there. I need to run to the lab and check on them."

A hand was extended to me, and I extended my palm in response. I followed him out of the office and shut my door and walked to the lab to see a few of my chemists work and collaborate.

I picked up a pair of gloves and goggles and went to check on Mitchell, one of our longest working chemists at Newton Industries.

"How's it going, Mitchell?"

"Hey, Blaze. Everything is good."

"What are you working on today?"

"A few DNA cell tests."

"I received your proposal."

"What do you think?"

"We can possibly pull it off, but you'll need to pick two assistants."

"I think Debbie and Brian would be good." He pointed to the junior chemists I'd hired a year ago.

"As long as you feel good about everything."

"Did you decide on opening a new lab?"

"Broderick is going to run the numbers to see if we can

use the money I won to have the proposal on the DNA and the lab will be good to go."

"Sounds great. Thanks, Blaze."

"No thank you. Without you we couldn't run this place. I'm heading to lunch, but you can text if something comes up."

"Will do."

Chapter Twelve

Ava

*T**he same day in California.**

"Wow," Melody said.

"Double wow." Trisha stirred the spoon in her ice cream.

"Yeah, had me ready to give my Social Security and bank account number."

"Damn. Blaze Newton?"

"Yes, and I keep thinking about him."

"So call him."

"No, I can't."

"Why not?"

Trisha wanted to hang out, and I'd been stuck catching up at work since we'd gotten back from Miami, so Melody and I came to meet her at the ice cream shop. Since we finished the workday, I had plans on hanging with my family since I was back in town.

"For one I hate him."

"You hate him but fell on his dick," Trisha muttered low, and I tossed my napkin at her.

"Shut up, Trisha."

"What? It's true."

"You're supposed to tell me *You're right, don't fall on the dick.*"

"Come on, it has to be better than Peter."

"Peter is reliable."

"Until you run out of batteries, late at night drinking a glass of wine and watching Denzel on *Training Day.*"

Melody and I burst into laughter.

"Please, don't sit up here and act like him playing that cop didn't get your lower lips tingling."

I cackled at her. "What should I do?"

"The sex was good, and he saved you from getting your ass kicked." Trisha pushed her ice cream away.

"I was holding my own okay, but this one—" I pointed at Melody.

"Diego is still pissed at me about that night. I had to suck a lot of dick."

"What!" Trisha giggled at Melody.

"Seriously, he was like *Melody, you need to sit your ass down.*"

"Maybe I need to go to Miami next time." Trisha threw her trash away.

"Blaze is a good guy. He can be an asshole sometimes, but he's like a brother to me and Diego's best friend."

"Where does he live?" Trisha asked.

"Boston," Melody and I answered at the same time.

Trisha grinned, pulling the straw from her soda up to her mouth.

"Have you researched your future husband?"

"He's not my future husband, and second, I slept with him once after being locked up in jail."

"Girl, you were in there for less than an hour, calm down." Trisha snickered with Melody.

I shoved Melody in the right shoulder. "It's your fault I went to jail."

"Sorry. Trisha, that was a difficult time for our friend, she's still dealing with trauma from the girl smacking her on the head," Melody said teasingly.

"Oh my God! Melody, you're a fool."

"You two will be put on the back burner of my emergency contact list," I fussed.

Melody wrapped her arms around my shoulder and kissed me on the cheek.

"Ahh, come on friend. We're sorry."

"You're young, Ava. No kids. You meet a guy, have the best orgasm of your life."

"Three." I held up three fingers.

"He made you come three times that night?"

I nodded my head, covering my face.

"Yes."

"Does he have a brother?"

"We didn't get that far."

"I know that's right, friend. Test drive him first." Trisha slapped hands with me.

"He's an only child," Melody answered.

"Besides, it would look weird if I dated him."

"How sway?"

"He's a competing chemist." I jumped up and threw my trash away.

"Not like you two will do much talking about science in the bedroom."

"More to relationships than sex, Trisha."

"Ughmm... Well, let me be quiet."

"She's such a dirty slut, right?" Melody giggled and tapped me on the shoulder.

"That's our Trisha," I joked.

"The queen of make it work with what you have, baby," Trisha replied.

Buzz!

"Oop, that may be your little boo thing," Trisha commented.

I stood up, gathered my purse, and slid my phone out. We were leaving, and she was about to come to my parents' house with me.

Mom: When are you coming to dinner?

Me: On my way now.

Mom: Bring me some beer.

Me: Ma really?

Mom: Yes, I need a bud light and some cigarettes.

Me: I thought you quit?

Mom: I thought you minded your own business.

Me: Goodbye lady.

I closed out of my phone and put it back in my purse.

"That woman drives me crazy."

"Who?"

Melody pushed the door open, and I sauntered to my car.

"My mom."

"What does auntie want now?"

"Girl, her beer and cigarettes."

"Mrs. Johnston is hilarious." Trisha tapped the window, and I unlocked on my side so she could climb in and buckle her seatbelt.

"See you at work tomorrow and think about Jamaica," Melody called out.

"Oh that bet. You still haven't decided on Jamaica?" Trisha asked.

"I'm not going." I hit reverse, backed my car out of the

parking space in front of the shop in WestLake Village, and turned the wheel, pulling off to the light.

"Why not a free trip?"

"We haven't spoken since I've been home."

"Hmnn. The phone works both ways, ma'am."

"Whose side are you on?"

I made a right at the light to head to the corner store.

"Always yours, but you need to have a little fun."

Beep!

"Please don't tell me my gas light is on."

"Pull over here at the gas station."

As I navigated to the first open spot, I pulled up, turned the car off, left the keys in the ignition, grabbed my purse, and took out my wallet. Trisha handed me ten dollars.

"What's this for?"

"Bring me iced tea and hot chips."

"I'm not your personal shopper."

"I'll pump." Trisha held her hands under her chin and smiled.

"Lucky you, my friend."

I unlocked the door and stepped out, sauntered to the door, pushed it open, and walked to the aisle with the chips and candy. I picked through what Trisha liked and picked up the biggest bag of hot fries, strolled to the drink section, and looked for her favorite Arizona iced tea.

"All this sugar," I mumbled to myself as I walked up to the cash register and dropped everything on the counter.

"Can I get forty on number five, please," I said.

"Sure," the gas attendant replied.

Chime!

"Put your hands up and give me all the money in the register!"

"Argh!" the attendant screamed.

I backed up out of the way and prayed he didn't shoot me. Just my luck to come into a gas station and get robbed. Next time I'd let it run out of gas and call a car service.

"Hurry up and give me the money!" he snarled, throwing the bag on the counter. He kept the ski mask over his face, but I could see he wore fresh new Jordans on his feet, had full lips and dark oval-shaped eyes, and smelled like that expensive Marc Jacobs cologne. I was attracted to a bank robber.

"You, with the curly hair, give me that watch and the money from your wallet."

"But—"

"Don't make me use this." He pointed at his gun.

I scrambled to remove my watch and tossed the money from my wallet on the counter.

"What else you got in there?" He snatched my wallet.

"Please just let me go."

He stared at me, and I started to feel uncomfortable.

"You look familiar."

"No I don't."

He smiled and the attendant glared at me.

"I have no idea who this man is."

"You're that scientist chick, right? Man, I loved you on that show."

"Uhmmm."

"Let me get your autograph."

"What!"

"Give me your autograph. Can't wait to tell my boys."

"Aren't you in the middle of robbing me?" I pointed at the gun.

"Yeah, but I won't hurt you."

The attendant passed the bag over to him, and I held my hands up in the air.

"You told me not to drop my hands."

He motioned for me to put them down and tapped the window on the counter.

"Give her a pen and paper."

"Sure, sure."

"Maybe this isn't a good idea."

"You're good, come on. Make it out to Mayhem."

I gulped, took the pen, and scrambled on the piece of paper.

"What should I say?"

"To Mayhem, my number one fan." He cackled, and I chuckled, forgetting I was standing with a lunatic.

"Here you go."

He picked up the piece of paper and nodded his head.

"Good looking, you got a boyfriend?"

"If I say yes will you kill me?"

"No hard feelings, I'm an honest man."

I dropped my hands to my waist and rolled my eyes.

"Nice doing business with you." He tightened his hold on the bag and ran back out of the store.

"Call the police!" the attendant told me.

"Can I get my gas first?"

* * *

Trisha was so animated at the dinner table I wished I'd left her ass at home and come to my parents' house alone. My mom, cousins, aunt, and dad were all sitting around enamored with her story, and I wanted to just forget this ever happened. I picked up the baked tilapia and greens to fill my plate.

"I see she forgot my beer and cigarettes," Mom scoffed.

"Ma, I was just robbed."

"You still had time to grab my things."

"Daddy."

"Baby, you know your mother." He passively shrugged his shoulders.

"Oh my God, you guys should have seen him. He was cute, with dreads," Trisha explained.

"Really, Trisha?" I pinched her on the shoulder.

"Sorry. I didn't know he was robbing the place. All I saw was a guy walk in the store."

"He wore all black with a ski mask."

"I thought it was the new fashion thing," Trisha replied, slapping hands with Kianna.

"Baby, pray about it, that's all we can do." Aunt Geraldine sipped on her mojito and cut into her fish. She was church-going and Bible-toting, all about saving yourself for the right man, but quick to gamble, smoke, and judge others on how wrong they were living their lives. Geraldine was my mom's older sister, married to my uncle Titus, who never really spoke up. They were Kianna's parents, a close family that had dinner at least once a week.

Kianna pretended to gag, and I giggled when her mom shot her an angry glare.

"Geraldine, stay out of these folks' business," Titus fussed as he unbuckled his belt and sat back in the chair.

"Shut up, Titus," Geraldine replied.

"So what did the police say?" Kianna questioned, changing the subject.

"Nothing, just be grateful I had my ID and he didn't take any credit cards."

"Well, that's good. See, Jesus works all the time, honey." Geraldine raised her hands up and mumbled a prayer. Trisha, Kianna, and I looked at each other.

Is she for real? Trisha mouthed.

Kianna nodded.

"Tell us about this Miami trip, Ava," Mom asked.

"I lost, but the winner gave me half the money."

"Why did they do that?" she probed.

Was I going to tell my mom I had a one-night stand in Miami with a guy I couldn't stand in the first place?

"He was just being nice."

Her eyes narrowed at me.

"Now what man you know is going to give you that much money?" She smacked Geraldine on the arm.

"Ma."

"Your mother's right, baby. What did he want in return?" Dad investigated.

"Nothing. We both worked really hard, and I knew him from around the science community."

"She worked him hard," Trisha muttered, and I nudged her to shut up.

Kianna laughed, but my parents stared at me.

"Did you sleep with him for money?"

"Huh?"

"If you can huh you can hear."

"No."

"It was after jail," Trisha pointed out.

"Jail!" everybody in the room shouted.

I dropped my fork and rubbed my temples.

"When did you go to jail?" Dad asked.

"Not a big deal, Daddy."

"Ava Johnston, you go to Miami and end up in jail, sleeping with a stranger and tell us it's not a big deal?" Mom remarked.

"When have you been the morality police?" I mumbled.

"Oop." Trisha sipped her iced tea.

"Better get your daughter."

"See, that's why I put you in private school, so you don't turn out like that." Geraldine motioned a thumb at me.

"Mommy," Kianna quipped.

"Hush, Geraldine. Maybe she went through a ho phase," Titus barked.

"Uncle Titus, I'm not a ho."

"It's okay if you is, baby. That's how your aunt got me." He calmly patted me on the hand.

"Titus, shut up and eat your food." Geraldine picked up the plate of green beans and filled his plate.

"First off, I'm not a ho. Secondly, I'm grown."

"Like mother, like daughter," Geraldine mumbled, motioning at my mom.

"Where's my cigarettes?" Mom rose up out of the chair, and Trisha cleared her throat.

"I'm going to head out. This was a lovely dinner. I'll talk to you later, Ava," Trisha commented, and I glared at her.

"Are you staying the night, baby?" Dad asked.

I sighed and nodded my head.

"Yeah, I don't feel like driving back home."

"Your mom cleaned your sheets in your old room."

"Thanks."

"We're going to head out too. Tell my sister I'll call her later." Geraldine hopped up and picked up the plate and grabbed the aluminum foil and wrapped it up.

"All right, Geraldine," Dad said.

"I'm leaving too. Call me later, Ava, we can do a girls' night," Kianna said.

"Okay, talk later." I stood and hugged her and Uncle Titus.

All three of them left the house, and I started to pick up the plate of food and take it to the kitchen.

"She's proud of you, baby."

"I know, she just drives me crazy."

"Join the club," he chuckled.

I wrapped up the pans of fish and greens and placed them in the fridge. I walked back to pick up the empty dishes to start washing.

"Go to bed. I'll clean this up."

"Are you sure?"

"Yeah, I like to clean up sometimes."

"Why?"

"'Cause your mommy gets turned on, and I get a little something extra at bedtime." He wiggled his brows, and I felt my stomach get queasy.

"You could have kept that to yourself, Daddy."

"Don't knock it till you have a husband and he starts doing house chores."

"All right, the visuals are too much. Good night."

"Night, baby."

Chapter Thirteen

Ava

Two days later.

"Yes, Henry!" Mom shouted, and I jumped out of bed for the second day in a row and ran to the bathroom to get dressed and leave. Since the robbery, I'd stayed at their house and commuted to work, but now, I was for sure going back home. I thought they'd slow down with that mess while I was here, but come to find out, my parents got it in every chance they got.

"Oh, Jamie!" Dad growled.

"I need a therapist." I rushed to wash my face and brush my teeth. I turned to get the shower water on, went back to the radio in the corner, and turned it up to drown out the noise and prayed they got the hint to stop.

Bang! Bang!

A loud knock from upstairs hit the wall, and I knew it was time to just leave the house and not even worry about a shower.

"Fuck this. I'll do a ho bath."

I grabbed the towel and washed under my arms and legs, sprayed on deodorant, and picked up the underwear out of the drawer, grabbing pants and a blouse. I quickly changed, pulled my hair up in a ponytail, picked up my purse and shoes, shut my door, and ran down the stairs. I heard the door of their bedroom shut as I gripped my hand around the knob of the front door.

"Ava! Are you leaving?" Mom asked, coming down the stairs.

I cleared my throat. "Yeah."

"You weren't going to say goodbye?"

As I held my eyes shut, I turned around.

"Girl, open your eyes. I'm decent."

I popped my left eye open and sighed in gratefulness that she wore clothes.

"Bye."

"Where are you going?"

"To work."

"Well, all right. Be safe and call us when you make it home."

"I will."

"Give me a hug."

"Uhm, have you showered?"

"Ava, you came out of my pussy."

"Momma." I groaned.

She extended her arms out, and I slowly went in and tapped her on the shoulder with one arm.

"How do you think your daddy and I keep it fresh?"

"I don't need to know this at eight in the morning."

I looked back up from my watch.

"Momma taught you everything you know." She shifted her hips.

"Gross."

"Bye, child."

I twisted the knob, opened the door, and shut it behind

me, shaking my head as I jogged to my car and tossed everything in the backseat.

* * *

An hour later, I tossed my purse on the chair and slugged down in the chair, kicking off my tennis shoes and putting on my Crocs.

Knock Knock!

"Here's your vanilla almond latte extra hot." Melody stepped in my office and sipped on her coffee.

I reached for the second cup.

"Thank you. I needed this bad."

"You look like shit."

"My parents."

"What did Jamie do this time?"

"Morning sex."

Her face scrunched up.

"Eww."

"Exactly my thoughts."

Melody stood at my desk.

"How are you feeling about the robbery?"

"Fine now."

"That's a scary thing."

"I'm going back home today."

"I got the check cashed and started interviewing people."

"Perfect, any prospects?"

"A few—at least two or three that stand out."

"I'm going to the community center to take the donation in a few weeks."

"I want to be there with you."

"That's fine."

"We have the distribution paid up and ordered more supplies."

"I was thinking of having a girls' night tonight."

"Who would be there?"

"Just Trisha, you, and Kianna."

"I have to fly out in a few days."

I stopped drinking.

"I forgot about that."

"You should think about going."

"That would open up too many things."

"Tell me you don't need a vacation and haven't thought about Blaze once?"

I rose up and picked up my white coat, sliding my arms inside and tucking my loose hair underneath.

"He probably has a date already."

"He doesn't."

"Have you been talking to him?"

"Diego is his best friend, and they keep in touch."

We started to walk out of the office to the lab, and she hit the button on the wall that opened the double doors. I grabbed the gloves on the counter and goggles.

"What about visiting him in Boston?"

"That would seem desperate."

"You had sex with him, right?"

"Yeah but—"

"It was good sex?"

"Melody, not here."

"Nobody here but Alyana."

Alyana was sitting in the chair with her headphones on staring into a test tube with ingredients.

"Still would rather not have my business out in the public."

"Promise me this."

"What, Melody?"

"You're single, beautiful, and smart. You deserve to have fun. Think about it before you decide to say no."

"He's probably moved on, anyway."

I sat in the chair next to her and picked up the bottle of alcohol and water.

"No excuses. Be spontaneous for once."

"Yes, Mother."

"At least your mother lives life to the fullest."

"How did we become friends again?"

Melody chuckled, lifting the wash bottle.

"You know I'm right, and besides if your mom is having more sex than you, that's a problem."

I couldn't argue with that point, but Blaze was probably not even thinking about me.

"Did I tell you I have to do the reunion show?"

"When is that?"

"In a few weeks."

"Back in Miami?"

"We don't know yet. Probably."

"That would be amazing if you two go back and you're a couple."

"You've probably picked out our kids' names." I laughed.

"Yep, two kids."

"Don't make me call Diego on you."

"He agrees with me."

"Not my friend Diego."

"Yeah, and I think you should go to Jamaica."

"Everybody has a word to say about my love life."

"Lack of love life, boo."

* * *

After work, I ran back home and cleaned up to prepare for the girls to come over and hang out. I ordered pizza, tacos, burgers, and junk food. I made sure nothing would cause my allergies to mess up. I loved my condo that overlooked the city and held everything from a media center, tennis court, gym and business office that I could use. Living out of the city of Los Angeles came with benefits from less traffic and more room to a lower cost of living. I poured the ice in the bucket, picked up two more bottles of wine, and set up tequila for margaritas. I'd told everyone to wear their pajamas and bring a change of clothes because I didn't want anyone to drive home.

Beep! Beep!

"Coming!" I shouted at the front door. I dropped the bag on the counter and picked up the two margaritas and walked to the door, dancing to Beyonce as I put one drink down and opened the door and smiled.

"Welcome to my home."

"Alcohol, yes!" Trisha grabbed the drink out of my hand.

"We've been here multiple times. Why does she think we need an introduction?" Kianna joked, taking the margarita off the desk.

"Come in and help yourself to the food."

Trisha lifted the bowl of chips and sat down on the couch wearing *Golden Girls* pajama pants and shirt.

"I saw that same outfit and wanted to get it at the store."

"So comfortable."

"So spill the beans on your life," Kianna questioned.

"Why do I have to start?"

"Because you're hosting the girls' night." Melody had on a black silk short set.

"Diego let you out the house wearing that?" I asked as

she took off her trench coat and hung it up. Melody bent down and took a piece of pizza and sat down next to Trisha. I went to the kitchen and grabbed the wine bucket.

"Diego was asleep when I left." She grinned, sticking her tongue out at Trisha.

"Put it on him and let him fall to sleep. I like your style," Trisha joked.

"He's going to kick your ass when you get home."

"Nope, because I have a change of clothes in the car." She poked her tongue out at me.

"All right, stop stalling. Are you going to Boston?" Trisha queried.

"I don't know." I sipped on my drink.

"Why not? You already tested the dick, and besides, nobody else is knocking on your door that you want to scratch that itch like Blaze," Kianna commented. I heard what she was saying, but I wasn't the spontaneous type of person. I thought practically about every situation, and if I show up and he rejected me, I'd look like a fool.

"I can tell by that look you think he'll reject you, right?"

"Why wouldn't he? I gave him the evil eye at every chance I could."

"But you made up for that by popping that coochie on him."

"If Geraldine heard you now."

"Girl, Momma will live," Kianna answered.

"How is Caleb doing?" I asked about her coworker and friend.

"Good. We have a concert to get ready for next month," Kianna replied.

"Kianna, your momma and daddy are hilarious, and I thought Ava had it bad," Trisha teased.

"Just imagine us growing up with them. So embarrassing," I said.

"Let's do a vote," Melody blurted out.

"What's the vote?"

"You should go to Boston and throw caution to the wind."

"When did you three get a say in my life?"

"Well, I'm your cousin, so you have to see me," Kianna remarked.

"We're your best friends and we love you. Besides, we're tired of you looking sad since you've been home."

"I'm not sad."

"Baby, you're strung out on that man and refuse to see it for yourself." Trisha slipped another chip in her mouth.

"I thought I could count on a single girlfriend to support me."

"I'm single too, but hell if you can get steady sex, why blow it up?" Kianna grabbed a plate of tacos.

"Who thinks Ava should go to Boston? Raise your hand," Melody asked.

Trisha put the drink down and raised both hands. I giggled, and Kiana raised both hands, along with Melody.

"I can't take time off from work."

"Yes, you can. Besides, I'll put someone else in charge," Melody spat.

"No more girl nights at my home."

"Just remember to ride that thang all on the beach." Trisha sat up and pretended to hump the pillow on the couch.

I cackled at her antics and covered my head in my hands.

"Maybe you need Jamaica more than me."

"I mean, we could make it a girls' trip," Trisha suggested.

"What if we all come back with a guy?" Kianna brought up.

Melody waved her ring finger in the air.

"I'm married already, but you three have fun catching you a husband," she answered and ate another pizza slice.

Kianna turned the music up on the radio, and we started dancing to Mariah Carey. I couldn't stop laughing as Trisha explained her latest date dramatics.

"Seriously, the man pretended to leave his wallet in the car," she complained.

I jumped up and walked to the kitchen to grab another tray of tacos, glancing over at my vibrating phone.

American Airlines: Your flight is scheduled for five am.

I smirked and closed out of the text thread of the reminders. This was going to be a big step not only for me, but hopefully Blaze wouldn't reject me. Diego sent me his phone number and the address of his apartment. I hadn't told the girls because I didn't know if he would accept me just showing up without notice.

"Come on with the tacos, Ava!" Kianna called out.

"Here I come." I put my phone back down and picked up the last five tacos on the tray and walked out of the kitchen.

"Have you decided?" Melody asked.

I laid the plate down on the table. "Let me sleep on it." I sat down on the floor and crossed my legs.

Chapter Fourteen

Blaze

Knock! Knock!

I poured the coffee in my cup and sipped the crisp, fresh, lightly sweetened drink I needed to function every morning. I checked my watch to see who could be here at my house knowing I had work right now.

Knock! Knock!

I put the cup down, strolled to the door, and peeked through the window, a surprised expression marring my face. I unlocked the door and opened to her smiling with a bag in her hand.

"Ava."

"Hi, Blaze."

"What are you doing here? How do you know where I live?"

"Can I come in?"

I saw the cab pull off, and I stepped to the side and let her come in and put her bag down.

"You have a nice home." She walked over to the fireplace and picked up the picture on the mantle of me and my parents.

"Thanks."

"I guess you're wondering what I'm doing here."

"Pretty much." I crossed my arms.

"I like you."

"Okay."

"I would like to take you on a date." Ava fiddled with her hands.

"Hold up. You flew out to Boston to ask me on a date?"

"Something like that."

"What changed your mind?"

"Honestly I realized the moment you defended Sharon you weren't so bad. Then we kissed."

"What are you doing with the bag?"

"I hoped you still needed a date in Jamaica."

I walked up to her and pressed my open palm to her cheek.

She smiled.

"I was thinking about dinner. You know the best places to eat."

"How about I give you a tour of my city, then dinner?"

"Sounds good to me."

"Ava Johnston, would you go out on a date with me?"

"Nope."

My smile dropped.

"Blaze Newton, would you go out on a date with me?"

"I'd be honored."

"Now I left Peter at home, so before we go anywhere, I think we need to make up for lost time." She reached up and grabbed the back of my head. I dipped my legs low and picked her up, and she wrapped her legs around me. Running her finger across my bottom lip, she pressed her lips to mine, sucking my top lip in her mouth. I gripped her ass, walked her back to my bedroom, and pushed the door open, running a hand underneath her dress. She stroked my beard, and I laid her on the bed, lifted off my shirt and started to unbuckle my pants. I dropped them on the floor, stepped out of them, reached for her left leg, and feathered kisses up to her inner thigh. Then I captured her lips again and slid my tongue inside, pressing my shaft covered by my boxers to her mound.

"Let him out to play." Ava reached down, slid her hand in, grabbed my member, and rubbed up and down. My eyes connected with hers, and I slid an index finger into her sex and matched her strokes.

"Blaze! Faster."

Beep! Beep!

"Shit! I forgot I had eggs cooking on the stove." I kissed her again on the mouth, removed my hand, jumped up, and ran to the kitchen, where I saw smoke rising off the stove.

"Do you have a towel or something?" She fanned it.

I reached for the hand towel off the counter, picked up the skillet, set it in the sink, and turned the water on.

"Sorry your breakfast messed up."

Ava stepped to the sink, still wearing her dress.

"That's fine. I'm hungry for something else anyway."

"I can cook. Oh my."

I lifted her dress, dropped to my knees, slid her panties to the side, and sucked on her pearl.

"Just like that," Ava cried out.

I buried my face in between her walls like it was my last meal alive.

"Arghhh... Fuck."

Her panties were in the way, so I ripped them off and lay down flat on the floor.

"Sit on my face."

Ava stood over me with her legs on both sides, and I helped her squat down, hovering over my face backwards. She reached and grabbed my dick out of my boxers and covered him with her lips.

"Ava, you taste so good, baby."

Ava rolled her hips, and I bit along her inner thigh, slurping on her juices.

"Shit, suck me faster." I smacked her left, then right butt cheek.

Her head went up and down, she rotated her grip as she massaged my balls.

"God, Blaze!" she shouted as I stuck a thumb in her ass.

"Fuck me."

I groaned, humping her face.

"I need to be inside of you now."

"Mmmmm..."

"I forgot the condom."

She reached down and removed a condom.

"Where did you get this?"

"It was in your nightstand. I grabbed it and put it in the pocket of my dress."

Ava rolled the condom on my dick and sat up, sinking down on my hard girth.

"So tight," I mumbled and planted both hands on her hips.

Her center was warm, fit my nine inches perfectly, and I could be wrong, but she was all into this just as much as I was. There was no turning back. I eased her down a little and sat up with her still in my lap and helped her to roll her hips as I pushed from below. My right arm went around her chest and gripped her breasts. Ava turned her head and plunged her lips to mine, placing her hand around my neck.

My index finger on my left hand went to her pussy lips, playing with her clit. The rush of her nectar flowing down made it even easier for the tug of war.

"Blaze, don't stop, I'm coming." Her eyes were closed tight.

I sped up my pace and planted another finger, and that opened the door for her. She convulsed in my arms and dragged her nails into my thighs as she came.

"Yes, baby!" She breathlessly let loose, and I filled the condom up, hugging her tightly around the waist. We kissed for a few more minutes and then stood up. Ava snatched a paper towel off the counter and removed the condom.

"That made me hungry."

"Let's shower, and then we can go find something to eat."

"Okay." Ava helped me to stand up, and I gripped her hand, kissing her palm.

* * *

The first place I thought of when wanting to eat was Menton's near the seaport district. After another round in the shower, we dressed and finally made it out of my house and drove to Menton's as we talked.

"You grew up here?" Ava questioned.

"For the most part. Originally from New York. Parents moved here for work."

"What do your parents do?"

"Dad is a salesman, and my mom works as a teacher."

"Sounds like you had a great childhood."

She rubbed the back of my neck as I drove.

"I did. My parents knew I had a love for science and encouraged me to pursue it in college."

"My parents were all about me trying different majors before I settled."

"How long have they been married?'

"Thirty years married, together over thirty-five."

"My parents have been married for about thirty-two."

"This place is beautiful."

"It's especially beautiful at night."

"Have you picked out a tux for the wedding?"

I pulled into A Street and Thomson Place and parked.

"Since it's on the beach, we don't have to wear suits."

"That sounds beautiful."

"My cousin is letting the bride plan everything. He's just ready for the party." I chuckled, got out of the car, and jogged around to let her out.

"Men and weddings."

We locked our hands together.

"At least he was honest about not wanting to be involved."

I held the door open and waved to the hostess. It was two of us.

"Hello, welcome to Menton's. We have a table near the back."

"Thank you."

Ava had looked the place up online to see the dress code was business casual, and she wore a similar outfit as the day at the cast dinner. It was form-fitting, a short dress that accentuated her curves.

"We'll have the waitress with you shortly." The hostess placed the menus on the table.

"Thank you."

"What do you suggest I have?"

"Do you trust me?"

She closed the menu and stared into my eyes.

"At first I would have said no, but since getting to know you in and out of the bedroom, I can honestly say I trust you."

"Then I'll order for you."

"Nothing with peanuts. I have allergies."

"I remember you wearing shades inside the hotel the first time I saw you in Miami."

"The prior night I had a bad reaction. I broke out in hives, and my throat almost closed."

"Glad you told me."

Ava leaned her arm on the table.

"What do you like to do besides work?"

"Pretty much like to travel, try out different restaurants, and hang out with my friends."

The waitress arrived and filled our glasses with water.

"Hello, I'm Hayley. What can I get you to drink?'

"Two white wines, please."

"Two white wines, any appetizers?"

"We'll have summer salad, beef tartare, and lobster mushroom." I closed the menu and passed it to Hayley.

"Great choices."

"Oh, Hayley. Can you make sure the chef cooks the food without mixing peanut oil, or mixing up the knives? My date has an allergy to peanuts."

"Of course, Mr. Newton."

"Oh, so you've come here before," Ava investigated.

"A few times. I can tell you right now, yes, a few women have been in and out as casual flings. But no girlfriend."

"So I don't need to worry about Sharon."

"No."

"She hasn't reached out?"

My hand extended to grab her palm.

"Today is about you and me. Sharon is not a topic of conversation."

Our hands clasped together.

"Tell me more about you."

"Pretty much work, hangin' with my friends, and trying to avoid my parents," Ava joked.

"Why do you avoid them?"

"My dad is cool, but they were young when they had me, and they still act like they are in their late twenties."

"Oftentimes we have to separate our parents from who we think they are and the people that they are."

"Tough sometimes."

"Agreed, but they were just like me and you once."

"Try waking up in the middle of the early morning from your parents fucking loud."

"Damn."

"Yeah, I got robbed and stayed with them."

"Hold up, you got robbed?"

"Not a big deal."

"To me it is. What happened?"

"Actually funny because he recognized me from the show." Ava laughed and slapped her hand on the table.

"Ava."

She cleared her throat.

"Sorry, I stopped to get gas and went into the station near my parents' house."

"He robbed you at gunpoint?"

"Yeah, then asked for an autograph."

"Wow."

"Yep, so I stayed with my parents for a few days before I went home."

"Here we go with your salad and beef tartare. The

lobster will come out soon." Hayley pushed both plates in front of us.

"Thank you."

"Did he take your whole wallet?" I probed.

She shook her head.

"No, just the cash inside and ran out."

"Did they catch the guy?"

"I doubt they even looked."

"How is your salad?"

"It's good. Try some." She picked up a small amount on the fork and reached out to feed me.

"Mhmmmm...tastes as good as you."

She blushed.

"Keep that up and you'll have me for dessert," Ava muttered.

"I'm not against that."

"Mr. Newton, you're not what I expected."

"What did you expect?"

"A jerk. Self-centered, cocky." Ava tapped a finger against her cheek.

I chuckled at her answer.

"Tell me your real thoughts, Ava."

"That was my first thought, plus hearing you talk at some conferences. But I know now you're funny, sweet, sexy, and still an asshole sometimes."

"Glad you gave me the chance to see behind your initial thoughts."

"Well, me losing and you still helping me out played a part."

"How so?"

I dropped my fork. I hope she wasn't about to confess she liked me because of my money.

"Before you freak out, it's not what you think."

"What do I think?"

"That it was about the money, and it wasn't. You showed a different side of yourself in Miami, and I appreciate that. You made me feel safe and protected, even when I was a little tipsy at the party. I grew up with a man that taught me to always be respectful when you find the one for you."

"So I'm your one."

"What do you think?"

"No fake relationship."

"I'm at a point if I'm dating I want it to be toward a future."

"I agree. So Ava Johnston, will you be my girlfriend?"

Ava dropped her knife, stood up, swished over to me, and bent down to kiss me on the lips.

"Mhmmm."

"That's a yes," she said.

"I want you to try this lobster and then I'm going to take you home."

"I'm all yours, Mr. Newton."

Chapter Fifteen

Ava

A day later.

Blaze opened the door of his lab, scanned his badge, and let me walk through security in front of him as I admired the size of his building. Newton Industries sat on a lot of acres. The building was white and brown, with the logo of Newton Industries in black on top. At least three stories high with a large parking lot blocks from universities.

"This is beautiful."

"Thanks."

"How long have you had this building?"

"A few years. I plan on opening another one."

Blaze pushed the button for the elevator.

"What floor is your office on?"

"The top floor. We have four floors."

The elevator door chimed, we hopped on, and he stepped behind me and hugged me around the waist, burying his face in my neck.

"We can't do this on the elevator."

"The boss can do anything."

"You're terrible."

He turned me around and kissed me on my forehead, then bottom lip.

Ding!

The doors opened, and we stepped off. I followed behind him to his office.

"Elene, this my girlfriend."

"Hello, I'm Elene, Mr. Newton's assistant."

His assistant was an older woman with long, gray hair and glasses that reminded me of my aunt Geraldine.

"Nice to meet you, Elene. I'm Ava Johnston."

"He finally brought someone worth bringing here," she told me, and I giggled.

"Elene."

"It's true. You've had some questionable women come around," Elene chastised him, and I covered my mouth and turned my head at her scolding him.

"Any messages?" Blaze asked.

"No, but Broderick emailed you an update," Elene said.

"Here's my office." Blaze tugged my hand, and I switched to his office as he unlocked it with his badge. I scanned the room and took in the décor.

"Nice office." I dropped down on the couch.

He walked over and sat down next to me.

"Thanks. Elene did the decorating."

Blaze stretched his arm on the back of the couch.

"You have a lot of work to do?"

"A few emails, but I want to show you our lab."

"Not scared I'll steal your secrets?"

"I have something you can steal." Blaze took my hand, placed it on his groin.

"I like your glasses." I changed the conversation.

He told me when he worked at the office he needed his

glasses, and I could see he was more than handsome with or without them.

"Maybe we can role play teacher and student?" He wiggled his brows.

"Mr. Newton, I was late today. Is there anything I could do to make up for being late?" I laid a hand on his chest, pretending to be a college student and he was the professor.

"Ms. Johnston, this isn't the first time you've been late."

Blaze gripped me by the shoulder, leaned into me, and bit me lightly on the cheek, sucking on the sting.

"You shouldn't go in there!" Elene shouted, and the door burst open. Blaze accidentally dropped me, and I tumbled to the floor. He reached over to help me up.

"How many times do I have to call you?"

"What are you doing here, Kenya?"

I looked between them both as I smoothed down my dress.

"Who is she?" Her nose was turned up in disgust.

I extended a hand toward her.

"Hi, I'm Ava."

She ignored my hand, and I shrugged.

"We have nothing to talk about, Kenya."

"Should I leave?"

"Yes." Kenya kissed her teeth.

His nostrils flared.

"No, Kenya is leaving and no longer going to just drop by."

"Blaze, we need to talk. I miss you," Kenya purred.

"Kenya, we haven't seen each other in months. I have a girlfriend now."

I waved, and she chuckled.

"When you're ready, I'm here for you." Kenya spun around and swished out of his office.

Blaze kissed my cheek, grabbed my hand, walked me to his desk, and sat down.

"Let me guess. Ex–booty call?"

"A casual thing, nothing serious. Come here." He tapped his lap.

I grinned, dropped to my knees in front of him, angled for his belt buckle, and exhaled a long-held breath. Some people might say I should have pressed him more on the woman, but I couldn't judge, because I'd had steady hookups with guys. When I moved out of my parents' house and became more comfortable with my sexuality, I knew what I would tolerate and not. Fighting over a guy is one thing you'll never catch me doing. If it was meant to be, he'd know where he wanted to be.

"Found something you like?"

"Very much like."

"What are you going to do with that?"

"Before I explore him again, do I need to worry about that?" I pointed at the closed door.

He picked up his phone and typed something, then put it back down.

"Blocked."

"Now I'm ready to feel something warm down my throat."

Blaze helped to release his dick, then tapped it against my lips, and I slowly twirled my tongue around the tip. I spit on the top, stroked his length to the base, and watched his reaction as his head flew back and he grabbed my hair tight to work my movements.

"Yo, Blaze." Somebody once again burst in his office.

"Fuck!" Blaze shouted, and I froze in place.

"What's wrong with you?" the guy said.

Blaze rubbed the back of my head, and I scooted under his desk farther.

"Broderick, I told you about busting into my office," Blaze hissed.

"So? I do it all the time."

The front of his shoes came into view, and that let me know he was sitting down in a chair.

"I'm busy."

"Doing what?"

Blaze cleared his throat.

"Ava, meet Broderick," Blaze called out, and my hand went up and waved.

"Oh shit! My fault. I'd shake your hand, but you're obviously occupied." He chuckled.

"Fuck you and get out."

"No problem. Nice to meet you, Ava," Broderick said.

I cleared my throat.

"You too, Broderick."

The door shut, and Blaze fixed his pants and stood up, reaching to help me stand.

"Sorry about that." He pressed a kiss on my forehead.

"An eventful day. Can I use your bathroom?"

"Yeah. It's through those doors." He pointed behind me.

"After that I want a tour of your lab."

Blaze nodded, planted both hands on my waist, and kissed me on the lips.

"We're not finished," he mumbled a few inches from my mouth.

"Anytime, playboy."

I brushed past him and headed to the bathroom.

* * *

Blaze held the bags of food in his hands as he unlocked the door of his home, and I followed while talking to Trisha and Melody on the phone.

"His lab is really nice."

"Was he surprised when you showed up?" Trisha questioned.

Blaze set the food on the counter and removed his jacket.

"He was, and I met his little girlfriend."

Blaze mashed his lips together, and I cackled.

"Girlfriend!" they both yelled, and I pulled the phone from my ear.

"Kenya."

"Ooh, was she pretty?"

"She was cute."

I took the forks and knives out of the drawer as Blaze grabbed the plates.

"Do we need to fly to Boston?" Trisha probed.

"No." I laughed, and he palmed his chest.

"Melody, where's Diego?" Blaze called out as he stuffed some ribs on his plate and then green beans.

"In his man cave," Melody blurted out.

"When are you flying down to Jamaica?" I investigated as I took some potato salad out of the container and kicked off my shoes. Blaze removed two bottles of water out of the fridge and carried our plates to the dining room table.

"Our flight leave tomorrow afternoon," Melody remarked.

I took two paper towels with me.

"We'll meet you at the resort when we get there," I replied as I headed to his bedroom.

"Okay, text me when you get there."

"Back to the Kenya chick," Trisha complained.

"She's not important." I laid the phone down on the bed and removed my dress, sauntered to the bag of clothes, and slid into some shorts and a T-shirt.

"Did you curse her out?"

"No. Why would I do that?"

"Make sure she knows not to mess with you."

"I've never been the fighting type. Besides, Blaze made it clear."

"Well, still. Keep an eye on her."

"Something else happened."

"Spill it!'"

"I was trying to give a blowjob, when his friend—"

"Was he cute?" Trisha asked.

"Trisha, I was under the desk."

"You could have popped your eyes up for a second," Trisha complained.

"Anyway, I was a little in the middle of things. Then bam."

"I would be so embarrassed," Melody said.

"I've done worse," Trisha blurted out.

"Like what?"

"Sex at a sporting game, and we accidentally got on the jumbotron," Trisha confessed.

My eyes blinked repeatedly, and my mouth opened and closed, not able not able to comment.

"How did that happen?" Melody questioned.

"All you need to know is that Dodgers baseball banned me for life," Trisha answered, and I laughed as I headed back to the living room.

"I can just imagine, but his house is beautiful."

"Send us pictures."

"Melody has been here before, but I'll grab some photos for you, Trisha."

"Have fun with your new boo, and call when you make it to Jamaica." Melody disconnected the call, and I dropped my phone in my pocket and entered the living room, sitting next to Blaze on the couch while he watched basketball highlights.

"What are you thinking?"

"I think today was fun, the trip here and you showing me around."

"But?"

"I'm going with you to Jamaica and then back home to California."

"Long distance."

"Yeah. We should talk about that."

"We will, but not now. Let's enjoy our time together."

I ignored the emptiness in my chest at the thought that I would have to part ways with him after the trip to Jamaica and sat back with his arm around my shoulder as we prepared to be in the moment even though our lives were on polar opposites of the country.

Chapter Sixteen

Blaze

Two days later.

I spent the two days laid up with Ava. We pushed our flight back because I wanted to have those moments from the office that we didn't get to have because of interruptions. One thing I'd forgotten to tell Ava about was that my family, mostly my aunt Kennedy, was a handful. Uncle Bernie let her do whatever she wanted. She prided herself on being the head of the family and my dad's older sister, so her ego was bigger than the president's. She clashed often with my mom when I was growing up and finally my dad told her to back off or he'd never come around for family events. So she calmed a little bit, but since my cousin announced he was getting married to the same type of woman, I knew this would be an over-the-top wedding and I prayed she didn't start with me about being single and try to hook me up with somebody. She was the one that had introduced me to Kenya, and I'd regretted it ever since that day.

"It's beautiful here, Blaze." Ava dropped her camera on the bed and stretched out. We'd just gotten into the resort, and I'd upgraded our room to a suite. My aunt gave all the family basic rooms, and I asked my dad if he cared, but he didn't want a fight with my aunt.

"A beach right outside. You know what that means."

"No I don't. Tell me." She gripped the back of my head and snuggled her face to my chest.

"Sex on the beach."

"Sand in my ass crack." She leaned back, smirking.

"Tomato, tomahto." We both laughed.

"First let's meet your folks, and Melody is probably wanting to shop."

"That's cool. I'll warn you now, my aunt Kennedy—"

"The mother of the groom is crazy. Promise she's nothing like my mother."

We grabbed our things and keys and walked out of the resort and saw the elevator. Five minutes later we stepped off, I wore a blue and white short set and Ava had a matching V-neck, strappy dress that flowed at the bottom with flat sandals.

"There they are." I pointed at a group of people arguing near the door. My mother and aunt were going off about something, and my dad looked to be ready to leave already. I approached my cousin Samir and shook hands, hugging him and then his bride-to-be, Skyler.

"Hey, folks, what's with the long faces?"

Mom smiled and leaned over to hug me.

"Nephew, glad you could finally make it. I mean, the flight tickets cost so much and you show up anytime," Aunt commented, rolling her eyes.

"I bought those tickets, Auntie."

"You don't have to explain anything to her," Mom told me.

"This is my son's big day. He could have ruined everything," Aunt fussed.

"How, Kennedy?" Mom hissed, balling her fist up.

"Just because you didn't teach your child about timely attendance—"

"Clay, you better get your sister," Mom spat, and I stepped in between them because we'd be here all day.

"Who is this?" Aunt lifted her index finger at Ava.

"My girlfriend."

"Hi, I'm Ava." She reached to hug my aunt, but she blocked her hand.

"Who is your family?" Aunt investigated, narrowing her eyes at Ava.

"Uhmm, Johnstons."

"Johnstons, never heard of them. Are they from the Midwest or the Hamptons?" Aunt lowered her shades and peered at Ava, starting from her shoes up to her hair. My girl shouldn't feel like she was under a microscope when my own parents weren't even asking all these questions.

"Auntie, you grew up in the Bronx."

"Watch your mouth, Blaze." Dad scowled, flashing a hard stare.

"But she—"

"Listen to your father, Blaze. Besides, I can handle your aunt," Mom said.

"Handle me! Please. I would never lower myself to your standards, Diana," Aunt barked, glaring back at Ava.

"Ava, you ready to shop?" Trisha, Melody, and Diego came up, and I groaned. Things would only escalate from here.

"Let me guess, that's your little posse," Aunt Kennedy remarked, and Trisha's head jerked back.

"Listen, you old geriatric—"

"Trisha!" Ava shouted, covering her mouth.

"You can't talk to my mother-in-law like that." Skyler's head whipped around.

"I'll talk to anybody I want to, Miss Fashion Nova Reject," Trisha insulted her outfit.

"I knew this was a mistake. I told you, Samir, to keep the guest list to the immediate family that I approve of." Aunt Kennedy's nose chucked up in the air.

"Girl, ain't nobody think about you," Trisha joked, and Melody giggled.

"Good because you're not invited." Aunt Kennedy pursed her lips, whipped around, and strolled to the van that would take us on the tour.

"Should we go?" Ava questioned.

"No, don't worry about her. She's a bitch," Mom whispered, and my dad shook his head.

"Stop calling her that, Diana," Dad scolded.

Mom shrugged her shoulders, and I laughed.

"Ava, this is my mom, Diana, and my dad, Clay." I introduced them.

"Hi, nice to meet you both. I'm Ava Johnston."

"Nice to meet you, Ava. My son hasn't brought a woman around us before. You must be really special," Mom informed her, running a hand over my cheek.

"Thank God those weren't your in-laws," Trisha said.

"Why?" Ava questioned.

"Because I would have had to boycott this union," Trisha teased.

"How would you boycott?" I asked, following to get on the bus.

"Probably called the police on your aunt and had her arrested," Trisha stated calmly.

All of our eyes peered at her.

"I know people in high places," Trisha remarked.

"I believe her, actually," Ava said, sitting in the front of the van and pulling out the brochure. I sat next to her with my hand on her thigh.

"Sorry about that back there." The van started to pull off.

"It's fine, she's a little High-maintenance."

"A little."

"I mean, it's your family."

"What do you think about marriage?"

"Never really thought about it too much."

Ava peered out of the window, and I listened to her ramble on about the best spots to see.

"Everyone, I want to say thank you for coming out to celebrate my only son's wedding." Aunt held up the blow horn.

"Woohoo!"

"As you know, I'm very picky about the people my son dates."

Everyone groaned.

"Kennedy." Uncle Bernie held his hand up for her to stop.

"What? It's true. Before Skyler came along, my son had some questionable taste, like some other people." Her eyes landed on Ava and me.

"Kennedy, if you don't sit your narrow neck ass," Mom snapped and erupted in laughter.

"Clay, get your wife, man."

"You get yours first," Dad argued.

"What's your aunt's problem?" Ava whispered, dropping the brochure.

"She probably needs a little ass kick," Trisha muttered through the seats.

"As I was saying, I'm proud of him and Skyler. This weekend is about you two, and I hope you enjoy yourselves." Aunt Kennedy released the blow horn and sat back down next to my uncle.

"Ignore her."

The tour guide took back over and started to explain the different locations of the drive we'd be stopping by to shop and explore.

* * *

Later that evening, we came back to the resort and changed our clothes after hanging out with my family earlier in the day. Samir wanted to have dinner with just the young folks while our parents did their own thing. I was happy with that because I was close to hopping a flight back home.

"Are you dressed, Ava?" I slid my watch on and walked out of the bedroom.

"Yep. What do you think?" She twirled around, wearing a body-hugging dress that was cut low in the front.

"I think we're going to be late."

"What about dinner with your cousin?"

"He can wait."

Samir would understand why we showed up late, but I wouldn't miss the opportunity to be inside of her again and hear her screams when she came on my dick. Not to mess up her dress, I spun her around and unzipped it. It fell to the floor, showing that she was only wearing a thong and no bra.

"You knew what you were doing." I took in her sexy appearance in the red heels.

"We only have a minute, Blaze, before Melody knocks on our door."

She was right, so I grabbed my phone and texted Diego.

Me: Will meet you at the restaurant.

Diego: I thought we were riding together?

Me: Change of plans.

Diego: What?

Me: Some things can't wait.

Diego: Lol! Skyler will be pissed.

Me: Fuck her.

I tossed my phone on the dresser, placed a finger on the back of Ava's neck, and ran it down her spine.

"Sit on the bed."

Glad I had extra condoms here with me for this trip, I reached into my pocket and grabbed them before I removed my pants. I tore one open with my teeth and rolled it down my length and bent down to plunge my tongue in her mouth. A husky moan left my mouth, and I didn't understand what she was doing to me because no woman had the kind of power to bring me to this feeling of need and want. I liked being up under her and cuddling, just lounging around my place. Not even thinking about sex.

"She ready for me, baby?" I moved her thong to the side.

Ava writhed underneath my hold as I slid a second finger in her pussy. My dick was brick hard and ready to stroke her sweet, warm sex. Her hips thrust up as I sped up the Circling of my fingers. I removed my fingers and slid them in her mouth as she stared in my eyes, and I knew she was the one for me.

"Mmmmhmm..."

Ava grabbed the base of my dick and lined him up to invade her opening. I gripped both her thighs and let her control how much she wanted to take as I slowly rocked into her at an even pace.

"Baby, fuck me," Ava begged as she stretched her arms

out and arched her back. I took her left breast in my mouth, and her palm went around to the back of my head. The bed started to squeak as I thought of us being apart right after Miami and who she could have been with. The only thing I could agree with my aunt about was that when she loved you, she went hard for you, and I was the type of person that would move the world for the one I love.

"Arghhh... Fuck, this is for me."

Our skin slapped together, and I moved to her right breast, pinched, sucked on her neck, and devoured her lips.

"This mine, Ava?"

Her eyes rolled to the back of her head, and I hovered over her, sinking deeper into her walls and thrusting upward as she squeezed around my dick.

"Oh God! Right...there."

"Ughh... Shit, Ava."

Her hands gripped the sheets, and I froze, eyes tightened as I came right with her. We kissed, and I started to rock up again.

"We have to meet them for dinner," she muttered to me.

"I'm not hungry."

She laughed and pecked me on the lips.

"What about your aunt?"

That completely made my dick go soft, and I pulled back from her and smacked my teeth.

"Fine, let's wash up and meet for dinner." She held her hand out for me to help her up.

Ava picked her dress up and fixed her thong back in place.

"We won't be that late." Ava filled toothbrushes for us both.

"I don't care." I yawned.

"Don't go to sleep on me. Bad enough we have to deal with Skyler."

* * *

We held hands and waved to everybody as we approached the table. We were only about twenty minutes late, so I figured they just were now ready to order dinner. I held the chair out for Ava and sat next to her, placing my arm on the back of her chair.

"Sorry we're late."

"No worries. Ava, you look like you're glowing," Trisha teased, smirking.

"The showers here are lovely," Ava replied.

"Golden shower," Trisha coughed, and I chuckled.

"Eh...that's nasty," Skyler remarked.

"What's nasty?" Trisha questioned.

"Talking about sex at the dinner table," Skyler brought up, and I shook my head.

"Excuse me. I didn't know there was table etiquette for dinner talk," Trisha argued, lifting her glass with her pinky finger out.

"Trisha." Ava narrowed her eyes.

"Baby, just relax," Samir said.

"Samir, what do you do for a living?" Ava asked.

"He's a businessman like his father," Skyler said.

"Can he speak for himself?" Trisha barked.

Skyler rolled her eyes.

"I mean damn, he is a grown man." Trisha smacked her lips.

"Who are you again?" Skyler probed.

"Samir, it's lovely to be here in Jamaica. What made you decide to get married here?" Ava queried.

"My mom picked this place out," Samir answered.

"His mom has great taste, and she wanted to make sure we were happy." Skyler clung to his shirt.

"That's nice," Melody muttered, and Diego chortled, removing the glass of wine from in front of her before things ended up in a fight.

"I'm on my best behavior," Melody said.

"Yeah right," Diego responded, picking up his wine glass as the waitress approached.

"Hi, welcome to Montego Bay. What can I get you?"

"I ordered for everyone already. It should be coming out for reservation under Skyler Doyle," Skyler explained.

"Actually, can I ask what you ordered?" Ava questioned.

"The most expensive thing on the menu, of course." Skyler chuckled, and my cousin smiled and kissed her on the cheek.

"I understand. but I have an allergic reaction to peanuts," Ava informed her.

"Don't you have something that can help with that? I mean, I'd hate to spoil my dinner plans because you're picky." Skyler smacked her tongue.

"Little Miss High and Mighty, if my friend dies from something you ordered, we will have problems," Trisha fussed, and the waitress looked between Trisha and Skyler.

"It's fine, Trisha," Ava said. "Can you just bring us a salad?"

"After the dinner arrangements I made." Skyler huffed and threw her hand in the air.

"Please tell me you're not really marrying this girl?" Trisha interrogated, and my eyes grew wide.

"Who are you?" Samir asked.

"I'm—"

Ava held her hand up to stop Trisha from blowing up.

"We're going to just have the salad. I'm fine, Trisha."

"Okay, I'll bring the order out and get an update on your scheduled course," the waitress told us, then she turned and went back to the kitchen.

"What time is the rehearsal tomorrow?" I queried to cut the tension.

"Eleven," Samir said, kissing the back of Skyer's hand.

"How many guests are attending?"

"We invited about three hundred and fifty," Skyler answered.

Ava choked on her water, and Trisha spat her drink out on the table.

"I don't even know fifty people in my family. What the hell?" Trisha joked.

"Probably don't even know who your parents are," Skyler mumbled under her breath, and that set off more loud arguing back and forth. Then Trisha lunged over the table to hit Skyler, and Skyler reached back to punch Trisha and ended up hitting Ava. The night was supposed to be easy with us doing dinner and then a night of lovemaking again.

"Ouch!" Ava shouted.

I could only hope this didn't make Ava want to leave early.

Chapter Seventeen

Ava

"We'll have the parents of the bride come in after the groom," the pastor explained, giving a rundown of the wedding. Everybody was still annoyed from last night and barely talked to each other, and Skyler was shooting daggers at Trisha and me. She wore two coats of makeup on her face to hide her black eye, and I wore shades to cover mine. Trisha stayed back in the room, and I came to support Blaze since he had to walk down the aisle with the maid of honor. Nobody told his aunt and uncle because we thought it was best to not cause more drama and get kicked out. Even his parents didn't know what happened.

"Pastor Sawyer, is the timing okay? I know we talked about giving them twenty seconds." His aunt spoke.

"They have more than enough time, Mrs. Doyle," Pastor replied. The man looked worn out from dealing with her fifty demands. All I knew was that she'd flown him out with the family and he came personally from their church with a nice payment to do the wedding, but Mrs. Doyle was adding more and more suggestions and changing things up from what his mother told me.

"She's an old, grouchy woman, you have to ignore her," Mrs. Newton murmured, and I giggled.

"That's your sister-in-law."

"I don't care. The woman is a menace."

I chuckled a little too loud, and Kennedy glared at me.

"What happened last night?"

"Nothing. What do you mean?"

"Skyler has at least the entire Sephora store on her face, you have shades, and your other friends barely talked at breakfast this morning."

"Nothing."

"Lie to my son, not me, Ava."

I sighed and released a long-held breath.

"Skyler and my friend got into a fight, and I was a casualty." I dipped my glasses low and showed her my black eye that was barely covered by makeup.

"Did you get a good lick in at least?"

"Mrs. Newton." I chastened.

"What? If that was me, I'd lay her ass out."

"Blaze know you talk like this?"

"My son doesn't check me, I check him." She snapped her fingers, and I laughed.

A throat cleared.

"Sorry," I said.

"As I was saying, Pastor, before we were interrupted."

The outside was decorated in yellow and white roses, with white chairs lined up overlooking the beach. I had to give her some credit for having good taste in decorations, plus the photos of the dresses looked like they cost a million bucks.

"I want the guys to walk out on one side and meet the girls."

"Whatever you say, Mrs. Doyle," Pastor Sawyer answered, closing the Bible.

"Good, let me sit and watch you guys run through it one more time."

Blaze groaned and walked back down the aisle with the rest of the men up to the edge, and the music started up. Samir's groomsmen started to come down slowly and walk to the right side and then the bridesmaid. They formed a line and coupled up to approach the front. I smiled at Blaze as he winked at me.

"If you pay attention to the front you'd probably learn how to get a husband too," his aunt hissed. Diana flipped her off, and Mrs. Doyle turned around in a huff.

"Diana." Her husband spoke.

Sorry, she mouthed, and I almost peed my pants from laughing so hard.

The music stopped playing, and the pastor began to speak.

"We are gathered here today—" Pastor Sawyer started to say.

Buzz!

I shooed the bee away with the folded-up newspaper in my hand, but that only pissed it off because another flew in front of my face.

"Samir, do you take Skyler to be your wedded wife?" Pastor asked.

Buzzz!

I fanned myself with the newspaper. It was getting hotter while we sat outside. Blaze's mom held the smaller fan in her hand.

"Shit!"

Buzzz!

Three bees flew across my face, and then a wasp was waved off by Kennedy. It came to the back, and I saw it land on the back of her chair.

"I gotcha now!" I extended my hand in a tight fist to hit the wasp with the newspaper when Kennedy whipped her head around fast, got in my face, and I accidentally hit her.

"Ahhhhh!" Kennedy screamed, falling backward to the ground.

"Kennedy!" Mr. Newton shouted.

"Honey!" Bernie ran to her aid.

"Momma!" Samir yelled, running to his mom.

I jumped up to go help, but Bernie pushed me back.

"Stay away from my wife," he shouted, nudging me back.

"I'm so sorry, what can I do?"

"Call an ambulance," Pastor Sawyer directed security, and Blaze came over with a pillow to put under her head. He came over to my side and grasped my head, kissing my temple.

"It was an accident."

"She'll be fine."

* * *

Skyler shot daggers at me from across the room of the waiting room in the hospital. The wedding of her lifetime continued to be interrupted by me and my friends, and I wouldn't have felt bad if she wanted us to leave without attending. Blaze was in the back checking to see how his aunt was doing with his dad, but they did say she wasn't in serious trouble. It was a little precaution to keep her overnight. The pastor was sitting next to Mrs. Newton, and I was next to her with a worried expression. The hospital had told us only two people could see her right now, but her son and husband had pulled some strings to get Clay and Blaze to stay.

"Ava, it was an accident. Don't stress yourself." Mrs. Newton clasped her hand on my knee to stop it shaking.

"She probably hates me."

"No, she doesn't."

"Well, Skyler does," I whispered, and Mrs. Newton glanced at Skyler.

"Yeah, she's ready to curse you out."

The double doors of the patient area opened, and Blaze walked out.

"How is she?" Skyler jumped up.

"She's fine. A little headache." Blaze wrapped his arms around me and snuggled his hand in my neck.

"Can I go apologize?" I asked.

"No," Skyler spat.

"Skyler," Blaze replied, his eyes narrowed into slits.

"Your little girlfriend has done enough. I want her gone," Skyler argued, and I couldn't be upset with her request.

"Maybe she's right."

"Skyler doesn't run me. You're staying with me."

"Well, she can't see Mrs. Doyle." Skyler crossed her arms over her chest.

"I'm family, and I say she can," Blaze barked back. He took my hand and escorted me through the double doors and down the hall.

"You don't have to do this, Blaze."

"Skyler acts like she's in charge, but the ring ain't on her finger yet." Blaze knocked on the door, peeked in, and led me to Mrs. Doyle sitting up in the hospital bed with a scrunched-up face.

Beep! Beep!

"What is she doing back here?"

"Mrs. Doyle, I wanted to apologize."

"I'm pressing charges."

"Kennedy," Mr. Newton muttered.

"No, Clay, this tramp hit me on purpose," she barked, and I was taken aback.

"Auntie, I love you, but you're going to have to stop talking about my girlfriend like that," Blaze demanded, and I placed my hand on his chest to calm him down.

"I raised you, Blaze, and you're taking up her side." Mrs. Doyle started to cry.

"Please don't cry. I'll leave, and again I apologize. I was trying to kill a wasp," I hurriedly explained.

"Why are you still here?" Mrs. Doyle yelled and ran the back of her hand across her head.

"Time for you to go, young lady," Bernie said.

"Blaze, man, get your girl for real." Samir grasped my arm and nudged me to the door.

"Samir, take your hands off her. We're family, but you're crossing a line. If she leaves, I'm leaving."

"Son."

"Sorry, Pops, but I'm not letting Ava take the blame for Auntie's attitude this whole time." Blaze reached for my hand.

"Blaze, you're breaking my heart." Mrs. Doyle held her face in her hands and cried. Funnily enough, when she looked up, no tears fell.

"What do you want to do?"

"You should stay. I can hang with Trisha and Melody."

"I brought you here. We can do something together."

"All right, fine, the little hussy can stay for the wedding," Auntie argued, reaching for the nurses' button.

"We'll let you rest up." Blaze kissed her on the cheek, and she smiled evilly at me behind his back. He turned to me and linked our hands, and we walked out of the room together back to the waiting area. He reached to hug his mom and told her what happened.

"Ava, ignore that old hen. You're a guest of ours," Mrs. Newton said and hugged me.

"Thank you, Mrs. Newton."

"We're going back to the resort to sleep."

"I'll go tell your father. I might head back as well." Mrs. Newton walked off to the patient area. The pastor stood up, and Blaze explained the update on Mrs. Doyle and that the wedding might be delayed a few hours with her staying overnight.

"This is all your fault!" Skyler shouted, trying to charge at me.

"Ah, Skyler, back up. You don't want to get another black eye by my girl," Blaze remarked, and I turned my head as a smirk formed on my face.

"Whatever," Skyler spat and sat back down.

"Let's go, Ava." Blaze grasped my hand, and we walked out to hop in a rental to get back to the resort.

Chapter Eighteen

Ava

A week later back in California.

Once the wedding was over, we flew back home in opposite directions. Blaze recapped the wedding disaster on FaceTime to Trisha and Melody while I held the phone up. He was animated with his hands flying everywhere and his facial expressions in reaction to his aunt falling down.

"Show us again how she fell, Blaze?" Trisha cackled, and I shoved her out of my face. We were at my condo hanging out before we headed to the center to present the check, then we needed to get back to work. Kianna was meeting us there with the radio station to help raise awareness for the kids.

"How was work today?" I jumped up from the couch, went to the kitchen, and opened the fridge to grab a yogurt and a bottle of water. Melody was sitting in the loveseat typing on her cellphone.

"Busy. We had two experiments that tested well today."

I peeled the lid back on the carton of vanilla yogurt and dropped on the couch next to Trisha.

"That's great. Any news from your aunt Kennedy?"

Blaze held the phone up to his face, while lying down on the couch.

"She banned you from Thanksgiving." He placed his left arm behind his head.

"Maybe it was too early to meet your family." I pouted, sliding the spoon out of my mouth.

Trisha peered toward me.

"Never discredit yourself. Besides, my parents already love you."

"Even your dad?"

"He laughed about the fight with Skyler."

"What are you doing later tonight?"

"I have dinner plans tonight."

My brows raised.

"A cute girl I met in Miami lives in California, and I'm going to visit her tomorrow."

"Really!"

"I planned on surprising you, but I figured it's better to have you aware."

"What time do you fly in?"

"Tomorrow morning."

"I'll make sure to text you my address. Maybe I can get off work early." I looked at Melody, and she rolled her eyes.

"I won't interrupt your work schedule. I can get Diego to pick me up."

"She's going to be all luvy duvy now." Trisha groaned dramatically.

"Blaze can hook you up with one of his friends," I told her.

"No thanks, after meeting his cousin and aunt. I've had enough of the snobby crew," Trisha joked.

Blaze chuckled, and I shook my head, checking the time on my watch.

"Babe, I need to get going. Don't forget to text me later when you get home."

"Okay. Talk later, baby."

I disconnected the phone and placed it on the table.

"So were the groomsmen sexy?"

"It was cute."

"What about the ceremony?"

The day of the wedding, Kennedy was barking orders to the staff while the wedding party started lining up, and the music started as we stood. I had to give it to Skyler. She picked out a gorgeous wedding dress, covered in lace and form-fitted, in a mermaid style. She had her hair pinned back with the veil over her head. They walked down the aisle, and Skyler's father let her hand go and kissed her on the cheek. Samir stood next to her and smiled when he grasped her hands.

"We are gathered here to bring this couple together."

Pastor Sawyer opened the Bible and read through the vows they'd given him.

"If there is anyone that has cause for these two not to be married..."

"Samir!" a raspy voice called out, and everyone's head whipped around.

"Fuck," Samir cursed.

A woman with a large pregnant belly, with long red hair and large breasts in a short dress stood at the door.

"Who is that?" Skyler asked.

"Nobody." Samir focused back on the pastor.

"Security!" Blaze's aunt shouted.

"I'm not leaving until Samir comes home," the girl yelled.

"*Samir, is that—*" Skyler spat.

"*I'm his pregnant girlfriend.*"

"*Girlfriend!*" Skyler and Kennedy shouted at the same time.

"What happened after that?" Trisha asked.

"He somehow convinced Skyler to marry him and sent Shonda away," I answered.

"Kianna's arrived at the center now. We should get going," Melody explained, standing up.

I raised from my seat, picked up the yogurt, and threw it away in the trash. I ran to the bedroom and slid my feet into my sneakers and picked up my jacket. Gazing in the mirror, I left my curly hair down and touched up my gloss.

"I'm ready," I called out, lifted my keys off the key holder, and picked up my purse. Trisha held the door open, and I followed her and locked it.

* * *

Melody talked with the director of the center as she turned the car off and removed her seatbelt. She laughed at something funny he said. I leaned out of the window and waved at the kids standing at the photo booth near the DJ stand.

"Thanks again, Ava. You've brought a lot of attention here," said Lester, the director of the Long Beach Community Center. We climbed out and shut the doors, and Trisha headed to the kids playing basketball near the front entrance.

"Mr. Jenkins, you don't have to thank me. I remember being a kid here when I was younger."

We hugged, and he kept his arm around my shoulder.

"I tell you all the time to call me Lester."

Mr. Jenkins escorted us to the front entrance of the

building that sat one story high, around five thousand square feet. They'd built a small library by the football field in the back with a gym, computer room, and science lab. He was now able to get the kids into things that would keep them busy and off the streets and build up their minds for the future.

"Hard to do when I've known you all my life."

"I hear you. Melody, how are you doing?"

"I'm good, Mr. Jenkins, excited for today."

Kianna ran over to us wearing a shirt with the radio logo on the front.

"How long have you been here?" I asked.

"About a Half hour," Kianna responded, holding her hand over her eyes to block out the sun.

"It's a nice crowd." I scanned the people, parents, and reporters that had shown up.

"Some of them want to interview you, but remember we get an exclusive." Kianna moved to the side, waving for her camera guy to come to the front.

"Nothing personal, Kianna." I peered at her with a frown.

"I wouldn't do you like that. This is Brenda, our news beat announcer."

Brenda held her hand out to me.

"Nice to finally meet Kianna's cousin, the brilliant chemist."

"I wouldn't say brilliant."

"She's modest. My cousin is the best."

"Love the family support. Ava, I will just ask you a few quick questions," Brenda said.

"We can do it out here before the ceremony starts," I suggested, with the time running out on the kids needing to get back home before it got late.

Brenda prompted the camera man to focus on her, and I slid to the left side so we were not blocking the door with the big bow on top and signage.

"99.3 listeners, I'm Brenda T. Your girl is out here in the community hanging with some brilliant minds." Brenda panned over to me, and I waved.

The cameraman pointed to me.

"Today we're at the Long Beach Community Center with Ava Johnston, the runner-up in the show *America's Next Top Chemist.*"

"Thank you for coming out today."

"My team and I wouldn't miss this, but full disclosure: Your cousin suggested we have you as the person of the day because of the work you do at the center," Brenda explained.

"Kianna is the best and supports me just as much as I support her."

Kianna waved at the camera.

"Tell us what's happening with the show."

"Well, we've filmed the ending of the show, and the reunion is coming up."

"Can you give us a hint on what's to come?"

"No, they never tell us."

"Who are you looking to catch up with?"

"Everyone, surprisingly." I chuckled.

"Everybody wants to know are you and Blaze really dating?"

"You make it seem like we're some celebrity couple." I chortled.

"The way you two battled it out and kissed at the end."

"That moment will live on in history."

"Well, we won't harp on it so much, but today you're giving back, correct?"

I slid my hand in my pocket and pulled out the check for seventy-five thousand dollars.

"Correct. Today I'm donating seventy-five thousand to the center."

"What made you want to give back?"

"As a chemist, I wanted to show the next generation that it's possible. We sometimes hear about focusing on doing sports or music. But a career in science and health can be just as wonderful."

"We love to see it, especially women in STEM."

"Exactly, women in STEM are lacking or not as supported like other major biochemists."

"Thank you so much, Ava, for talking with us." Brenda extended her hand, and I thanked her back.

"Are you ready to do the ribbon cutting?" Mr. Jenkins asked.

He held the large pair of scissors out for me to hold, and I let Melody stand in the middle of us.

"We're ready. Here's the check."

"Are the cameras ready?" Brenda called out to her team.

"On the count of three," Director Jenkins told us.

All three of us held the scissors up to the ribbon.

"One, two, three!" the kids yelled out, and we cut down the middle.

"Yay!!!"

The entire crowd cheered and clapped, the doors opened, and we allowed everyone to come in and directed them to the signs on the wall directing them to the science lab. Kianna and her team filmed the kids running inside to see the different workstations with test tubes, small white coats, and goggles. The room was set up like our labs at CrimsonBio, with a few textbooks and boards with different chemistry facts.

"Ava, you've gone above and beyond for the kids." Director Jenkins pointed at the eight-year-olds that crowded around the board with the chemical breakdowns of making easy home tests of the elephant toothpaste.

"When are you going back to Miami?" Melody probed, helping me pass out coats to the kids. She held eye contact with me.

"In a few days. I knew when anyone wins they'd want to do a reunion episode."

"Are you flying with Blaze?"

"We haven't talked about flying down together, but since he's coming here we might as well."

"How is the relationship going to work long distance?"

"That's the big question. I don't know."

"Could you see yourself moving to Boston?"

"I'd visit, but my life and family is here." I rubbed the top of the head of a little boy that wore short dreads and glasses.

"Talk to him. You don't want to get deeper in love, and it's something you can't compromise on."

"I know."

"Stop, little girl!" Trisha shouted, and I glanced across the room as Trisha blocked a little girl from spraying her with a spray bottle.

"She's going to beat that child. Let me go help her." Melody shook her head and walked off.

"What are you thinking about?"

"Trying to figure out how Blaze is going to do with my parents," I told Kianna.

"He'll be fine."

"Definitely Jamie and your mom are the ones I'm really concerned about."

"We can always ship them off to a nursing home," Kianna teased.

"Please don't give me that idea."

Chapter Nineteen

Blaze

Another phone call from my aunt gave me a headache as I walked through the airport to head to the car as Diego waited for me. The flight down here was smooth, and I'd talked to Ava briefly on the phone about her day at the center previously.

"You have a responsibility, Blaze."

"Auntie, Samir is a grown man."

"He looks up to you."

"I can't help you."

She started in on my cousin having a side baby and what it would do to our family's legacy. I'd known what my cousin was doing behind the scenes, but I never spoke on it because it wasn't my business. One time I told him to be honest with Skyler, but he felt he knew better, so I left it alone.

"But I bet you helped that little hussy in California," she spat.

Honk!

I looked to my right and saw Diego's gray Range Rover at the curb near the pickup. LAX is a massive airport, and trying to get through was insane with the crowds and different signs directing traffic.

"If you don't want me to hang up, I suggest you stop talking about Ava."

She sighed. "When are you coming back? Does your father know you're out of town?"

"Auntie, I have to go, we're under a tu...nnel."

"Wait!"

I disconnected the call, opened the door of his car, threw my bags in the backseat, and climbed in the front.

"Your face was all screwed up. I guess that was your aunt?" Diego slapped hands with me.

"Man, that woman is so judgmental." I blew out a breath.

"Family."

"Sometimes we can't pick them."

"Are you going to my place or Ava's?"

"I'm going to your place until she gets off."

"Did she give you her address?"

"Yeah, but I'd rather not be there until she's home."

Diego turned the left signal off as he pulled into traffic.

"She and Melody got home late from the center."

"Yeah, she sent photos, and everything looked good."

I scrolled through the pictures on my phone of her and Melody.

"I have to ask."

"What?"

"Are you moving here?"

"I wanted to wait, but Broderick got the numbers together, and I can open a lab out here."

"For real?"

"Yeah, man."

"So you're settling down?"

"I mean, I need to talk with Ava and see where she's at first."

Diego continued onto the freeway.

"Only advice I can give is to keep your family out of your relationship."

"I'm meeting her parents while I'm here."

"Then you're heading to Miami, right?" he questioned and got over in the right turn lane.

"Yeah, just pray they're is nothing like my side. Well, my aunt at least."

"Her parents are more laidback for the most part, but her aunt Geraldine is a mess." He chuckled.

"Is she like my aunt?"

"Geraldine is like the do as I say type person in the church, but undercover she is smoking and drinking."

He laughed, and I grinned as he pulled up to a one-story home a few minutes later, turned in the driveway, and turned the car off.

"This is nice, man." I got out of the car and grabbed my bags. He locked the car, and walked to the front door and I followed, dropping my bags on the couch. Diego headed to the kitchen.

"Do you want something to eat or drink?"

"Just water is cool. I know Ava's getting off early so we'll probably do something."

He came out of the kitchen.

"Here you go." He handed me the water bottle. "Take a seat."

"Thanks. Ava told me her parents can be a little young in mindset."

"They had her in their early twenties."

"I get that. Probably making up for the time now that she's grown."

"Like I said, her aunt and uncle are really the crazy ones."

"We'll see."

"If you can handle your aunt, you'll be fine with her family."

"That's still debatable."

Ring!

My phone rang.

"Who—"

"What?"

"My cousin."

"Better answer before he leaves you messages."

I accepted the call.

"Blaze!" Samir yelled, and my forehead creased.

"Samir, what's going on?"

"Man, I need your help."

"What's wrong?"

"Shonda is out here fighting Skyler."

My eyes opened wide.

"She's pregnant."

"I know. Then my momma came over, and she's helping her."

"Wait, what?"

"Momma trying to kick Shonda out."

"Where are you?"

"I can't say," he mumbled.

"Samir! Get your ass out here now."

"Who is that?" I investigated.

"Man, Blaze, where are you at?"

"I'm in California."

"Fuck!"

"Calm down and explain what's happening."

"I went to spend the night with Shonda."

I growled. "Samir."

"I know, but she's carrying my baby."

"What about your wife?"

"She's on her period," he fussed.

"That's not an excuse, dumbass!" I shouted and dropped down onto the couch.

"Momma, go home!" Samir yelled.

What the hell? Diego mouthed, and I put the phone on speaker.

"Be honest with them both and go home."

"I'm calling the police!" Skyler screamed, and I heard loud banging.

"Skyler showed up with my momma. I guess Shonda showed her a picture of us on social media."

"What in the hell is wrong with you, man?"

"You are the one that made me do this."

"How the fuck is this my fault?"

"Nobody can live up to your perfect ass," Samir shrieked loudly.

I rubbed my temples.

"You're not putting this on me. Leave me out of your drama."

"Whatever happens, and I lose my baby and wife, you will have to live with that."

"No, you will have to live with that." I hit the end button and rolled my eyes. A grown-ass man that couldn't be honest with himself and the people in his life but blamed the problems on everybody else.

"He said it's on social media?" Diego questioned, picking up his phone.

"Yeah, she more than likely tagged Samir in something." I went to my personal page and typed in Samir's name.

@SamirDoyle taking care of home;)@Shonda&Samir

A screen shot of Samir in her bed sleeping with no shirt on.

@skylerdoyle not his baby@samirdoyle

"Your aunt must have passed out at these pictures right now." Diego laughed, and I wondered how this was going to play out at family dinners.

"This is why I don't deal with too many women."

"You're lucky Kenya didn't get too crazy."

"I told you she showed up at my office."

"Guess you're just better at putting your women in check than Samir." Diego showed a clip of Shonda trying to kick Skyler.

Ring!

"If this is Samir or my aunt, I'm blocking half the family." I groaned and lifted my phone to see Ava's name scrolled across it.

"Hey, baby," Ava said.

"When are you off?"

"Now."

"Are you on your way home?"

"I was thinking you could drop your things off at my place and relax before dinner with my folks."

"That's fine with me."

"Uhmmm."

"What?" I asked.

"Somehow I was tagged in your family's little squabble."

"Huh?"

"I guess Skyler found me on social media and tagged me with saying I hired Shonda to sleep with Samir."

"He just called me about them fighting."

"Yep. It's all over social media. Trisha talked to me about it and saw how she said I had set her up."

"You don't even know Shonda."

"I know."

"Just ignore them."

"I blocked them."

"Good. We don't need that negativity."

"I'm pulling up to Diego's house now." Ava hung up the phone.

I jumped up and hugged Diego bye.

"Ava's outside. We can catch up soon."

"All right, man. Be safe tonight," Diego joked.

My upper lip turned up at his comment, and I picked up both bags and walked out of the house. I saw her red Prius and smiled. She started to open the door, but I stopped.

"I got it, stay inside." I bent my head through the window and kissed her lips.

"I missed you."

"I missed you more. Pop the locks." I opened the back seat and dropped my bags in. I headed around to the passenger side and opened the door, climbed next to her, and lifted her chin.

"How was your day?"

"Not bad, now that you're here."

"Sorry about my folks."

"Not your fault."

"I'll make it up to you."

"I should be apologizing now."

"Why?"

Ava put the car in drive and headed toward her home.

"My family is just as crazy."

"We all got them in our family."

"So true."

"The donation at the center?"

"Yeah."

"You did a good job. Proud of you."

"Thanks. They loved everything we made."

"I want to donate some things as well."

"Really?"

"Yeah, some equipment we haven't used in a while we can donate."

"That would be great."

"Anything to help."

"Are you hungry?"

"Not really."

"You can shower at my place then we'll head to my parents'."

"Do they know I'm coming?"

"Yes, they know my boyfriend is coming." She grinned, stopping at a stop sign.

"How far do you live from Diego?"

"Not that far."

She hopped on the freeway, and five minutes later, we pulled up to the condo building.

"Nice place."

"Thanks."

"Can't wait to explore the amenities." I pressed a kiss on her lips.

"Since you're going to be dealing with my parents, I'll give you a little tip."

"Like what?"

"Bring alcohol." She laughed, I shook my head, and we got out of the car and went up to her place.

* * *

Ding!

Two hours and two orgasms later, Ava drove us over to

the liquor store and grabbed a few bottles of wine, then we made it to her parents' house in record time. They lived in Westlake Village in a modest one-story brick home that matched my parents' style with a two-car garage. The door opened, and a young woman with long braids and chestnut brown skin smiled back.

"Finally. Come in and save me from this torture."

"Blaze, this is my cousin Kianna," Ava introduced us.

"I've heard a lot about you, Kianna."

"Hopefully all good things." She pursed her lips at Ava.

"Of course I did, cousin."

I removed Ava's coat, then mine and hung them up in the closet that she pointed out.

"How is everybody?"

"Usual self." Kianna grabbed the bottles of wine.

"Remember, I'll give you a hand job later to make up for tonight."

"That's right, cousin, keep your man happy." They high-fived, and I chuckled while they headed into the other room. I saw pictures on the wall of Ava as a little girl wearing glasses and holding up trophies from a science fair.

"You won all these?"

She looked back at the wall.

"Told you I live for science."

"Ava, get in here and stop messing around!" a raspy voice called out.

Ava rolled her eyes. I grasped her hand, and we walked into the dining room and saw their family sitting around.

"Ma, you didn't have to yell."

Ava bent down and kissed her father on the cheek.

"Blaze, this is my father and mother. Mr. and Mrs. Johnston." Ava pointed between them.

"Ava has told me a lot about you."

"Funny. She left out a little about you." Mrs. Johnston spoke, and I went over to shake her hand.

"Have a seat, young man." Another older woman to my right spoke.

"Auntie," Ava hissed.

Her aunt shushed Ava.

Chapter Twenty

Ava

These two would be the death of me. I wouldn't feel bad if Jesus came down and knocked some sense into their brains. Blaze pulled the chair out for me, and I sat next to Kianna, who glared at her mother.

"Tell us about yourself, Blaze," Aunt Geraldine investigated.

She was the type that would ask Kianna's date for a DNA swab when she was younger in high school, heading into college.

"I'm a chemist like Ava and have my own business."

"Do you drink?" she questioned, while holding a glass of rum and Coke in her hand.

"Auntie!"

"Girl, be quiet. This is my job."

"I do occasionally, in social settings."

"You hit women? Because my niece and daughter learned Jujitsu," Auntie Geraldine said.

I covered my head in my hands.

"Ignore them," I whispered in Blaze's ear.

"I don't believe in putting hands on a woman, ma'am."

"Church?"

"I used to go when I was younger."

"And now?"

"He doesn't need to tell you his life story."

"Let your aunt talk, Ava. Besides, we have to know you're in good hands," Mom remarked, holding up the plate of Salisbury steak.

"Ma, that would be fine if your sister wasn't crazy."

"Hush, little girl. Henry, you have the talk about the birds and the bees with Ava."

"Ava knows about sex," my dad replied, and I could almost curl up in a ball and drink the rest of the night away at how they were behaving out of the gate.

"My sex life is not up for debate at the dinner table."

"Sex is important, Ava, and we need to know he's going to protect himself and not be out here on that hop from one girl to another," Mom complained.

"Ava and I are exclusive."

"See, we're good."

"Does he give you an orgasm?" Aunt Geraldine asked. Kianna choked on her food, and I dropped my fork on my plate.

"Daddy!"

"Geraldine, leave the boy alone."

"Don't talk to my wife like that. Ava needs somebody to look out for her," Uncle Titus argued.

"She is grown," Mom fussed back.

"If you would have raised her in the chair we wouldn't have had to always keep an eye on her," Aunt barked.

"Keep an eye on her."

"Jaime, you know how fast you were growing up." Geraldine threw her hands up in the air.

"Ava had a roof over her head, clothes on her back."

"We are not doing this at the dinner table," I argued.

"Yeah, Momma, you can't really talk. I mean, you preach about the church and then sin when it's over."

"Kianna, I know you're not sassing me."

"Kianna, be quiet," Uncle Titus barked back.

"What about that time Momma went out to the casino and gambled the rent money away?" Kianna confessed, and I giggled, covering my mouth.

"Shut up, Kianna," Aunt Geraldine told her.

Kianna shrugged her shoulders, and we clinked our glasses together.

"Anyway, Blaze, what are your intentions with my daughter?"

"I hope to be together as a couple as long as she'll have me."

"I'm not going anywhere." I kissed him on the lips.

"Long as you're not bringing any babies here. I'm too young to be a grandmother," Mom said.

"No babies anytime soon." She didn't look a day over thirty, but she was forty-six, and my dad was forty-eight.

"When are you heading to Miami for the reunion?" Mom questioned.

"Day after tomorrow."

"We're going with you," Mom said, plopping two tickets on the table.

"Please don't embarrass me."

"When have we ever embarrassed you, Ava?" Aunt asked.

All eyes stared back at her before the conversation seemed to change to Kianna working at the radio station and her mom disapproving as usual.

* * *

The next night Blaze held my hand as we walked down the street from having dinner together at my favorite restaurant, Crossroads. I wanted him to explore the city. We'd gone on a hike earlier in the day at the Hollywood sign, then we went to the beach and now we were ending the night at dinner with just the two of us.

"Tell me how you really feel about my family?" I stopped him, and we stood at the corner of the street.

"They seem protective of you, and that's great. Some people don't have that."

"Be funny we end up with crazy in-laws." I hugged him around the waist.

"Just imagine our kids being around them." He chuckled.

"You've thought about kids?"

He rubbed a hand down my back.

"I have. They'd have your curly hair and heart-shaped lips." He pecked me on the lips and pushed a piece of hair behind my back.

"So you've thought about marriage?"

"I think that's something I want to explore when we're both ready."

"How would that work if you live in Boston?"

Beep! Beep!

His face scrunched as he grew distracted. I turned to see what was so alarming.

"Oh my God! Hey! That's my car." I dropped my arms from around his waist and ran to the tow truck guy as he hooked my car to the bed.

"What are you doing?" I argued.

"You parked in a red zone," he remarked.

My eyes scanned the parking place, looked farther up at the corner, and saw a small piece of red section.

"That's barely red."

"Doesn't matter. You parked there."

"But—"

He passed his business card, and I snatched it out of his hand.

"YOU CAN'T BE SERIOUS!" I ran toward the front of his truck.

"Ava, we'll get your car out," Blaze yelled.

"No, Blaze, it's the principle. You can barely tell I was parked here."

"Ma'am, either move or get run over," the burly man with the long beard and scar over his eye yelled, closing the door of his truck.

"I'm not moving!"

"Ava!" Blaze shouted as he came around the front and tried to drag me off. I kicked the truck's front fender.

"Shit!" I hurt my toe when I kicked the front of the truck.

He laughed and honked his horn.

"That's what you get!" the driver shouted back.

"Asshole!"

"Calm down." Blaze chuckled, helping me over to the curb.

"That's not funny."

"I'll call an Uber to get us home."

"He's a jackass and could have easily let us go."

"Yeah, but you know how folks are nowadays. All about the money."

Blaze removed his phone and went to a car service.

"You think you'll make it home?" he questioned.

"I don't think it's broken, but maybe we should get it checked out."

"We can stop at the hospital."

"I can hear my parents now fussing about my being irresponsible."

"Don't worry about them."

He kissed my forehead.

* * *

The curtain was pulled back, and I lay in bed with my toe taped up because my dumbass actually sprained it from kicking the truck so hard. Blaze sat in the chair next to my bed and flicked through the channels as I waited. The door flew open, and Melody, Trisha, and Kianna ran in with worried looks on their faces.

"What happened?" Melody questioned, standing on the left side of the hospital bed.

"Who did this to you?" Trisha asked, standing on the right side.

"Please tell me who we need to curse out," Kianna said.

"Nobody to curse out but myself."

"She kicked a truck and sprained her toe," Blaze explained, and now hearing it out loud, I wanted to start the day all over again.

"Why did you kick a truck?" Melody sat on the bed.

"The asshole said I parked in the red zone and wouldn't release my car."

"So your car got towed?" Trisha investigated, and I nodded.

"Well, at least Blaze was there with you," Melody said as the nurse came in with a chart.

"Hi, how are we doing? I'm Nurse Betty." She removed her stethoscope, touched my wrist with two fingers, and checked my heart rate.

"I'm good. Can you give me anything for the pain?" I started scratching my arm, feeling a little Light-headed.

"Uhm, nurse?"

"Yes? You don't look so good."

"Ava? What's going on?" Blaze jumped up and moved Trisha out of the way.

Beep! Beep!

I started to feel my eyes dip low.

"My EpiPen?"

"Are you allergic to something?" The nurse started to look through my medical chart.

"Is she all right?"

Melody checked my purse and removed my EpiPen to give me a shot.

"I'm so sorry. I had egg rolls right before I came here from lunch," Nurse Betty begged.

"She's allergic to peanuts." Kianna smacked her teeth.

"Can you get someone else please," Trisha demanded.

Nurse Betty walked out of the room, and I started to get a better handle on myself.

"You go out to dinner and end up with a broken toe and a nurse that almost killed you."

"I'll be fine, you guys. Blaze is here." I scooted up in bed.

"I did call—" Kianna started to say.

"Where is my child!" My mom burst through the door, followed by my aunt with her Bible in her hands. Blaze was pushed aside as she fell on top of me dramatically, and Aunt threw some type of liquid on the sheets.

"What is that?" My eyes blinked repeatedly.

"Holy water," she quipped.

"I'm possessed."

She kept throwing it back on me.

"We do things in the house of the Lord." She patted my sprained foot.

"Ouch!" I cried out.

"Ooh, sorry, baby."

"Mother, have a seat please." Kianna pointed her to the couch in the corner.

My mom held her hand up to my forehead.

"What are you doing?"

"Checking your temperature."

"I don't have a cold. Stop."

Mom started moving the covers up on my chest.

"Tell us what happened," Dad asked.

"Daddy, I'm fine. Take them back home, please."

"Not until you're leaving." She scoffed, pouring me a glass of water.

"I'm leaving in the morning and then I fly out to Miami." I frowned and passed the water back.

"Henry, talk some sense into your daughter."

Mother went to sit next to my aunt on the couch.

"How about we let her handle things on her own?" Dad tried to stick up for me, but both women glared at him.

"I can assure you both, Ava is all right with me," Blaze informed them, and that could have been the worst mistake.

Aunt pointed at me.

"Where were you when this happened?"

"I—" Blaze went to answer, but she interrupted him.

"You probably did this to her. I told you he looked funny." Aunt Geraldine rambled on and tapped on her Bible.

"Yeah, they say the quiet ones." Mom goaded her on.

"Listen," Blaze started to say.

"Blaze didn't do this, and I want you both to leave now," I chided, crossing my arms over my chest.

Both of them rolled their eyes and stood up, with my father escorting them out.

"See you tomorrow morning then."

"No, I'm heading straight to the airport."

"With a broken foot?" Aunt Geraldine asked.

"A little sprained. I'll be fine."

My aunt pulled her Bible to her chest, closed her eyes, and mumbled underneath her breath.

"Amen." Aunt Geraldine placed her hand on my forehead, popped one eye open, and grinned.

"Amen." Mother followed her out of the room.

"Somehow I don't think that was meant to be helpful." Trisha was the first to answer.

"If I were you, Blaze, I'd check underneath my bed before I go to sleep," Kianna joked.

We all burst into laughter, and Blaze ran a hand down his head as he sat down in the hospital bed with me. I laid my head on his shoulder.

"I told you my folks are a mess."

He kissed me on the forehead. "I'm not going anywhere."

"You guys can go."

"All right, since you're in good hands. We'll be watching you on TV." Melody hugged me, then Blaze as the rest of the girls followed her out of my room.

"What do you think about me moving down here?"

I yawned, stretched my arms, and laid my hand on his chest.

"Move where?"

"Here to California."

"Really?"

"Yeah. I was talking with Diego, and I have plans on opening another lab."

"Will you move here permanently?"

"Yes. I love you."

That was the first time I'd heard him say the words out loud, and even though it was an awkward situation, I couldn't help but feel warm inside that he cared so much about me.

"I love you too. If you're sure that's your decision and no regrets."

"I mean, your aunt is making me regret a lot of things, but moving here to be closer to you is not one of those things."

Blaze picked up my chin and slid his tongue across my bottom lip.

"Mmmmm...I love you."

We kissed for the next twenty minutes, then fell asleep in each other's arms.

Chapter Twenty-One

B*ack in Miami.*

"Ladies and gentlemen, welcome to the live reunion of *America's Next Top Chemist*," Teddi announced, and the crowd clapped their hands. I wore a light beige chiffon dress with a black shawl over my arms. I was wearing one heel, with the other foot wrapped up and sat on the couch next to Kimberly. Blaze was on the opposite side with Joel, Andy, and Asher. The judges sat behind us with the large sign of Blaze's name on top.

"We're so happy to have everyone back with us today."

"Woohoo!" the crowd cheered.

"For judges, we once again want to thank the participants and support."

Sharon held the microphone up.

"Teddi, you know more than anyone I love to give back to the community," Sharon lied, waving to the crowd.

"That is true, Sharon. We'd love to know what you have been up to since the airing of the show."

"Well, what haven't I done?" Sharon nervously held the mic in her hand.

"I hear you've been approached to come back to judge a new season, of course?" Teddi helped her out.

"Exactly, coming back here, and recently I met up with Blaze about investing in his company," Sharon fabricated again, and I didn't trip on her attempt to rub his shoulders.

"Really? What have you partnered on?" Teddi questioned.

"I think what Sharon means is that she was looking to donate, and I told her about the wonderful work Ava is doing at Long Beach Community Center."

"Ooop! Shade." I heard a voice that sounded like Trisha.

"Donate," Sharon harped.

"Yes, that's right. Blaze told me you'd requested to donate ten thousand to the center."

The crowd started clapping again.

"That's amazing, Sharon. Isn't that correct, audience?" Teddi turned to the crowd.

Sharon glared at me with a tight smile and looked back up to the crowd.

"Kids are the future. You have to give back," Sharon answered as she pushed the mic into Danny's hands, and I smirked.

"Since the reunion, Joel, how has your life changed?"

"My life has gotten busier with more requests to do interviews on science issues," Joel answered.

"Did you expect to have such a huge following?"

"I don't think any of us expected that."

I nodded in agreement that more people were noticing us from the show.

"Blaze, you started the show focused on winning. What have you done so far with the prize money?"

"I invested in my company, and I'm planning on

opening another lab in California," Blaze answered, gazing at me.

Teddi caught his eye.

"Do you have something you'd like to announce, Blaze?"

"I'll leave that to everyone to figure out."

"Our show was watched by over twenty million viewers. How does that make you feel, Ava?"

"I'm glad people enjoyed the show and appreciated what we all brought to it."

"Do you have any family members here with you?"

The family I didn't invite but flew down as support and tried to drown me in holy water at the hospital.

"My family is here in the audience."

Clapping!

"How does it feel to see your daughter on TV?" Teddi asked as the audience wrangler moved the microphone to my mom.

"We've never been prouder of our daughter," Mom bragged and waved to the camera.

"Why are you talking to her? My nephew won the money!" a loud voice screeched out, and my mouth dropped open.

"Shit!" I heard Blaze mutter in a low voice.

I saw Joel lean into Blaze and mouth *his family*.

"Ma'am, who are you?"

"Clay, stand up and represent our family," Kennedy complained.

"Kennedy, sit down!" he fussed, and this was becoming even more wretched.

"I guess we have a family reunion on air. We'll be right back from the commercial." Teddi winked at the camera.

"Five-minute break!" Hair and makeup rushed over to us and touched us up.

"Did you know your family was coming?" I muttered across the room.

"No, which means everyone is probably here." Blaze started to walk off toward the audience.

"Blaze!"

"Blaze! We need you to stay in your seat. We're coming back," Abigail said.

"Three, two, one," the audience wrangler called out, and the clapping began.

"Live again on *Top Chemist* reunion, and we have Ava's family in the audience and now Blaze's family has shown up."

"Blaze's family should have been introduced first!" Aunt Kennedy fussed.

"We'd love to know how you feel about your son winning the prize money."

"He's my nephew, and I didn't want him on this show, but his mother insisted." Aunt Kennedy turned her nose up at the camera.

"Who is that?" Aunt Geraldine questioned.

"Someone that doesn't socialize with people that wear synthetic wigs," Aunt Kennedy sassed.

"Oooh," the audience said.

"I can guess the family dinners are going to be interesting this year," Teddi joked.

The audience laughed, and Teddi came back over to the stage, standing at the edge.

"Kimberly, you've been on the show twice. How have things changed?"

"At first I wasn't looking forward to going back home

without anything, but since then a lot of companies have come forward to donate," Kimberly explained.

"That's wonderful. We know how hard it is for schools and funding," Teddi replied.

"Asher came down to the school and helped us set up the fundraising event," Kimberly informed her, gesturing to him.

"This year was about changing lives, and we can see all of you have come into your own," said Teddi.

"Aaahhhh!"

"As a thank you, we've arranged for you all to have dinner together, and your families are welcome to join." Teddi happily pointed to the screen with a video of a fancy dinner at a restaurant in Miami.

"Thank you again for tuning in, and we'll see you back here next year for *America's Next Top Chemist!*" Teddi signed off, and the audience continued to clap hands and cheer as we stood and waved to the camera.

* * *

Bickering was blasting down the table, and I wanted to just be alone with Blaze and celebrate how we became a unit together, but having both families and friends here, it would have to wait.

"What are you throwing at me!" Aunt Kennedy held her hands up, trying to block Geraldine's holy water.

"Something that you've never experienced and need more than that tacky perfume!" Aunt Geraldine squawked, holding the napkin up to her nose to block out Kennedy's strong perfume, which was overtaking the entire table.

"Blaze, I refuse to accept these people in our family."

Aunt Kennedy glared at Geraldine, but my mom was drinking, ignoring them.

"This is a party. Sit down, we have photographers outside," Blaze demanded, scooting his chair up closer to the table.

We had my family on one side and his family across from us with the other cast members mixed around. I felt so embarrassed at the way they were acting because they'd caught a few shots of them bickering on camera. I didn't know if they would edit them out or use it as a blooper reel, but I knew people back in California would have a field day with the aunts' crazy antics. The waitress came around and started to fill our glasses with champagne, but my dad removed the glass away from my mom, and I said thank you.

"Henry, give me that back," she fussed.

"You've had enough, Jamie."

"Momma." I eyed her sternly.

"Jamie, you're embarrassing the family," Aunt Geraldine spat.

"Blaze, is this really who you've been hangin' around with?" Aunt Kennedy complained.

"Your nephew would be lucky to be in our family," Mom blurted out.

"I looked you up, and you shouldn't be talking about anyone's family with the blasphemy happening with your family!" Aunt Geraldine narrowed her eyes at Samir, Skyler, and Shonda all sitting together in the corner. I asked Blaze why she would have them come down here together, and he said after they got out of jail, Shonda agreed to drop the charges if she was brought into the family fold and given just as many rights as Skyler. To my knowledge, it had turned into a sister wife thing, but Shonda didn't mind because she wasn't planning on leaving

Samir anytime soon even with Skyler being a few weeks pregnant.

"My family has nothing to do with your niece and her lack of class," Aunt Kennedy hissed and chucked her chin up before she sat back down.

"Only thing you run is your son and his harem of women," Geraldine spat.

"Oooh, you and this dry wig can shove it up your—" Aunt Kennedy yanked her wig off her head and tossed it on the ground. Geraldine covered her head with both arms as gasps were heard around the table.

"Sit down or get out, both of you!" I leveled my gaze between them.

Uncle Titus picked up her wig and placed it back on her head backwards, and I couldn't help but burst into laughter.

"Uhm, you might want to turn your wig around. Slightly to the right," Trisha suggested, and that made the entire table ring out with laughter.

"You're buying me a new wig." Geraldine held eye contact with Kennedy.

"I mean, it's the least I could do," Aunt Kennedy replied.

"See? We can all get along," I said.

The food was catered in by the staff, and each guest was given either the choice of lamb or steak with a variety of sides. Blaze slipped his hand on my palm on the table and squeezed. I smiled and leaned into him, and he pressed a kiss on my cheek.

"I'm going to tell them now."

"About California?"

He nodded.

"Should I go hide somewhere?"

Our lips joined again.

"Only if I'm there."

Blaze cleared his throat and stood up.

"Everyone, can I have your attention?"

"Ma, put that down." I pointed to her wine glass.

She chugged it down.

"I have an announcement," Blaze said.

"Please don't tell me she's pregnant," Aunt Kennedy blurted out.

"For real, we don't believe in that premarital sex," Aunt Geraldine commented.

"I'm not pregnant," I chastised, leaning back in my chair.

Both of them released a breath.

"As I was saying, since coming to Miami, I've grown closer to Ava."

"That's right, friend, you went to Miami, got a man and money." Trisha snapped her finger.

I held my finger up to my mouth to be quiet.

"With Ava and me growing closer, I've decided to move to California and open a chemistry lab," Blaze announced, Aunt Kennedy fainted, and Samir passed the baby to Shonda and jumped up to help his mom.

"I'm fine, I'm fine. I had a terrible dream. Blaze said he was moving."

"He is, Momma," Samir said.

Aunt Kennedy's glare was harsh. "Clay, do you hear this? He's selling off his business for her."

"I'm not giving up my business," Blaze responded, sitting down.

Kennedy pressed her lips together.

I know women like her." Aunt Kennedy's gaze shifted to Shonda.

"I have my own money, and I would never ask him for anything."

"Exactly. My niece doesn't need anything from him. Besides, she's going to have a prenup," Aunt Geraldine quipped.

"Well, my nephew will have a prenup and post up," Aunt Kennedy insisted.

"You are jumping the gun. We're not getting married," I protested, picking up the knife on the table to start eating.

"I'm happy for you, son." Clay held his hand out to shake.

"Thanks, Pops." Blaze gave him a one-armed hug.

"As long as you're happy, Ava." Dad came around the table, and I stood to hug him.

"Thanks, Dad."

"Me too, honey. Just remember morning sex will keep it spicy!" Mom drunkenly told me, then her head fell down in the middle of the plate.

"Oh my God!" I gasped.

"See? It already starts," Aunt Kennedy murmured, pointing at the end table where my cousin Kianna and Dad were trying to help my mom sit up, wiping the sauce off her face and hair.

"This is better than the show." Joel continued eating.

"Shut up, Joel!" we all shouted.

"Did we ever find out about Peter?" Kimberly questioned, and I almost died of embarrassment.

Twenty minutes after cleaning my mom up, they carried her to the car and sent her back to the hotel, and I followed to make sure we got her in bed and cleaned. I left after kissing Mom and Dad good night and slid the key into the door of my room.

"Is she sleeping?" Blaze asked.

I dropped the key on the table.

"Yes, praise the lord."

Blaze wrapped his arms around my neck.

"Let's go to bed. We've had a long day."

"Okay. Did your family get in their rooms?"

"Yeah, everybody's good."

"Just imagine if we had told them we were getting married." I chuckled.

"We might as well get used to them as in-laws."

"Yeah, at least I can give it to your aunt. She does have better wigs." I laughed and removed my watch and coat. He sat on the edge of the bed, and I walked in between his legs.

"She has some good taste."

"We won't see each other for a month. What am I going to do without you?" I bent my head down to stare into his eyes.

"You'll be too busy with work."

"Never."

"Only a few weeks for me to wrap up things in Boston."

"You're right. The time will fly by fast."

Chapter Twenty-Two

Ava

Two *months later in California.*

He seemed to know the exact amount of pressure to lay on my pussy as his tongue ran from the back, his hand tangled in my hair. His husky voice caressed my ear. The moan I held was close and ready to come out in a scream of passion as I gripped the edge of the bed from the floor. He placed his other hand on top of mine and laced our hands together. The tease of his dick tapped on my opening and left again, slowly moving back in as my legs spread further apart. I dropped my head down, arching my back as he hit me with a sharp burst of thrusts. I turned my head, and his tongue swept onto my lips, parted them, and took me to a blissful edge. My eyes were dilated with lust at his powerful thrusts, the feel of his body on top of mine. His hands floated around to the front of my breasts, and my shallow breaths rolled out. Soon he removed himself and lay down on the floor. I gazed at the moisture on his shaft and licked my lips, going to taste the precum with my tongue. I held another finger to my clit and dipped two fingers inside as I licked up to the tip. His stomach tightened, his breath hitched, and his eyes closed.

"Please, keep going," he wheezed, moving my hair out of my face. His head leaned up, and I winked and moved the hand I'd used to play with my clit into his mouth.

"Faster, baby."

I did what he wanted and went down to the base of his shaft. My eyes started to water, but I held back from gagging and popped him out. I moved up to his mouth and sucked on his tongue and mounted him again.

"Hard and fast," I rasped out and placed my hands on his chest as I bounced up and down. The heat and pace went from zero to a hundred in a split second, and my breasts bounced in his face. He nearly chocked on them as he leaned up and pinned my arms behind me and bent his head. His thrusts continued, and my sex clenched when he slid a thumb in my ass.

"Oh, Blaze!"

"Wet and tight, baby."

"Ohh, you make me feel so good."

I heard a noise, and my eyes popped open.

"Blaze!"

He smirked, and I saw Peter in his hand.

"Only right we finish off with your little buddy."

Blaze slowly removed his finger and moved my vibrator to my clit, and I was lost as I clung to his shoulders, and a river washed over us.

"Ughh! I'm there."

"Fuck! Come like that again." Blaze shoved his tongue in my mouth, hair stuck to my face, eyes blurry and dizzy as he spilled his hot seed in me.

* * *

Two hours later, I dropped the box on the floor of Blaze's condo, which was two blocks from my place. Trisha, Melody, and Diego were all here helping him move in and get set up. The movers had brought in the bigger furniture, and we carried the boxes. I wiped the sweat off my brow and redid my hair in a high bun off my shoulders, watching him and Diego carry his boxes of clothes.

"Stop staring so much and help the girl," Trisha complained, throwing a pillow at me.

"Sorry! I deserve to take a little break." I stuck my tongue out.

Blaze dropped the boxes on the floor and came around to the couch and planted his arm around my shoulder.

"Trisha, lay off my baby."

"Thank you, baby."

"See, this is why I stopped helping people move," Trisha fussed, starting toward the kitchen.

"Stop being a brat. We're ordering food soon."

"Good, because Blaze lied about the amount of shit he has to move."

Trisha grabbed a root beer from the fridge.

"Only a few more left."

"I need to know what you are doing about your new lab," Diego asked, standing with his hand on his hip.

"The opening is in two weeks."

"Are you inviting your whole family?" Trisha wondered, and my eyes roamed around his tall stature and muscles on display in the cut-off shirt.

"My dad invited my family." Blaze blew out a breath and picked up the box of books and moved them to the back hallway.

"Well, I'll skip that event," Trisha chimed in and high-fived with Melody.

"Anyway, the building is nice that he picked out." I grabbed the pictures of the location off the table and shoved them in her hands.

"Nice. Are you going to work there?"

"No. I'm still going to work with Melody."

"Really? When your man has a lab here and can pay more?" Trisha waved a hand.

"She's right, Ava. You guys would make a great team."

"Are you firing me, Melody?"

"Wha! No, I'm not firing you, but it makes sense."

"What makes sense?" Diego probed, walking inside from the elevator.

"We think Ava should work with Blaze at his lab," Melody told him, and Blaze came from around the corner.

"That's too much pressure. He's already moved down here, and now you want to force him to hire me."

"You're the best in the business. What do you think, Blaze?"

"That's Ava's decision." Blaze stopped and placed his arms over his chest.

"You'll be tired of seeing me at work and then at home." I waved them off.

"Think about it at least. Besides, you and Blaze work well together," Melody commented.

I nodded and continued opening the boxes and putting things away in the cabinet of the kitchen. Trisha turned on the music of his radio, and we listened to Kianna's station 99.3 blast Drake's "*o to 100*" real quick. Trisha started dancing, and I laughed at her expression and went to stand beside her, mimicking the moves of her hips from left to right. I slapped hands with her as we bounced the words off each other.

"Get it, Ava!" Trisha encouraged me, and I twisted around, slid to the back, then slowed and started to move low and come back up.

"That's my favorite song!" I called out.

"Are we dancing or moving?" Diego remarked, breaking up our fun.

"Don't be a Party pooper," I snapped, throwing my hand on my hip.

"Blaze! The girls are messing around," Diego snitched on us, dropping the office supplies box on the floor.

"Stop being a snitch, Diego, before we call Aunt Geraldine with the holy water," Trisha teased, holding her palm on her chest.

Ring!

I took my cell out of the purse on the table and saw Geraldine's name scrolled across it.

"You rang her up." I showed her my phone, and Trisha cackled when I answered.

"Hello," Aunt Geraldine said.

"Hey, Aunt Geraldine."

"Ava, I had a dream, honey."

"A dream?"

"Yes, my dream told me to call and check in on you."

"I'm fine, Aunt Geraldine."

"Well, what about that boy you're dating?"

"He's fine. We're helping him move."

"Mmm...huh... Just remember your holy water, baby."

"Aunt Geraldine, I didn't tell you."

"What, baby?"

"Blaze doesn't believe in church."

"What! Titus, find my keys. We have to get over to Ava's right now."

I disconnected and turned my phone off, ignoring her calls.

"She's going to be on your doorstep with the whole congregation tonight." Trisha laughed.

"That's fine, because I'm sleeping here tonight."

Epilogue

Blaze

Six months later.

"Three, two, one! Congratulations." We cut the ribbon together at the joint lab A&B Biochemistry facility.

"Blaze, smile into the camera." Melody held her camera up in front of the two of us, and Ava held her badge in her hand with our company name.

"How many more are you going to take?" Ava investigated, dropping her smile.

"That was the last one," Melody lied and snapped another one as I dropped my arm from around Ava. I stepped back and looked at the front door of our brand-new business that we'd established over the past six months. Broderick had flown down and made sure all of the right documents were set. The building was in Westwood near the university, so we were able to hire some interns and assistants, and some of my employees from Boston came to work here with me, specifically Elene. I offered her the chance to retire, but she wanted a change of scenery.

"I think you guys did a great job," Kianna said.

Kianna had been able to get Brenda to come back and do an interview and tour of the facility, and that opened doors for contracts and research opportunities to come to our location.

"Thanks, Kianna. We appreciate you getting the station to come here again," Ava responded, hugging her cousin.

"This helps me more than you guys to build up my producing credits," Kianna answered.

"Has Aunt Geraldine forgiven me yet?" Ava asked.

Aunt Geraldine and Kennedy had become close friends throughout the past few months and even talked on the phone more, although she was still pissed at Ava about the joke she'd pulled. But she was cool with me outside of everything else.

"Ignore her. She'll get over that," Kianna said.

"What are your plans now?" Broderick strolled over and grinned in Kianna's face.

"Broderick, you can move away from my cousin," Ava hissed, grabbing Kianna's hand to move her to the other side.

"Ava, your cousin isn't bothered by me," Broderick told her.

"She doesn't know any better," Ava sassed, and Kianna laughed.

"Blaze, tell Ava I'm not that bad," Broderick begged.

I raised my hands up.

"I'm not in this situation. We all know you're faithful, bro."

"Kianna, you ready?" A guy stepped over to her. He was a few inches taller than her and looked annoyed by Broderick.

"Oh, Ava, you remember Caleb. Blaze and Broderick,

this is my coworker Caleb," Kianna introduced us and we shook hands. Broderick glared at him.

"Hey, Caleb, we haven't seen you in a while," Ava noted.

"Work is keeping me busy, and family, plus your cousin and her drama." Caleb pointed at Kianna.

"I don't have drama." Kianna pushed him on the shoulder.

"Okay, Kiki." Caleb rolled his eyes and threw his arms around her neck, released his arm nudged her away joking. Then headed back to the station van.

"Who's that guy?" Broderick asked.

"My friend," Kianna responded.

"Is something going on between you two?"

"Broderick, you've known my cousin for less than two days. Please find another woman to hound." Ava pushed him away and grabbed my hand as we walked into the building. Kianna headed over to the DJ booth and finished breaking things down.

Ava and I looked at the entrance of the lobby and security section and walked down the hall to our offices across from each other.

"Are you excited?" Ava pushed my door open and led me inside to the light brown decorations that matched my old office in Boston. I had a picture of us that sat on the desk from our kiss on the show.

"More than you can imagine."

She sat down on the edge of the desk.

"We should christen your office."

"This place is full of our family and friends."

"The door can be locked."

"Yeah, we don't need any more people walking in on us." Ava grinned up at me.

"What do you think our next chapter will be?"

"Who knows, but I can't wait to experience the minutes, hours, days, and years with you by my side."

"Like Trisha said, going to Miami was good even though I lost the contest."

"Why do you say that?"

"Something gained more than money can buy."

"Love."

"Love," Ava responded as she picked up the remote off my desk and pressed the button and the doors locked.

* * *

I hope you enjoyed Ava and Blaze's story. Check out sneak peek on Kianna and Caleb's story.

Do you love Second chance romance? Find Jessica and Joseph **"Heart of Stone Book 4" here** https://books2read.com/u/4NXyPG with a host of characters intertwined.

Follow Desiree and Gabriel in ***"Temptation?"*** It's a standalone contemporary, sports, curvy girl romance. Check it out here https://books2read.com/u/mle1Vv

Check out Mafia romance here: ***"Antonio and Sabrina Book 1"*** https://books2read.com/u/4AxKLo

Please also check out my **"Mutual Agreement"** https://books2read.com/u/mgzzWX, a steamy political romance.

Have you checked out **"She's All I Need"**? click here https://books2read.com/u/49lkeW a sports, opposites attract romance.

Sneak Peek: Something Earned

Kianna has worked hard and knows she deserves a promotion at the music label, despite what all the naysayers in her life say.

Caleb has gone above and beyond to prove he can handle taking on more responsibilities at work. What he's not sure he's ready to handle is competing with Kianna for a job.

A promotion is up for grabs, but only one can have it. With ex-lovers, a relationship that's blurring the lines between coworkers, good friends, and lovers, Kianna and Caleb have a lot on their minds.

Can they ignore the outside distractions and focus on what matters, or will they jeopardize what could be the best thing that ever happened to them?

What's Next?

Want to know what happens next?

Follow me on my website to catch the next release.

Reviews are the lifeblood of the publishing world. They're read, appreciated, and needed.

Please consider taking the time to leave a few words on your review platform of choice.

Sign up for updates and sneak peaks at the site below.

www.chiquitadennie.com

Acknowledgments

I appreciate all of my readers new and old because without every single one of you, I wouldn't be here doing what I love.

Catalogue of Releases

By Chiquita Dennie:

Temptation

The Early Years-A Prequel Short Story

Antonio & Sabrina: Struck in Love, Books 1, 2, 3, 4

Janice & Carlo: Captivated by His Love

Heart of Stone, Book 1: Emery & Jackson

Heart of Stone, Book 1.5: Emery & Jackson, A Valentine's Day Short Story

Heart of Stone, Book 2: Jordan & Damon

Heart of Stone, Book 3: Angela & Brent

Heart of Stone, Book 3.5: Jessica & Joseph Bottoms Up

Joaquin Fuertes (The Fuertes Cartel Book 1)

Cocky Catcher (A Hero Club Novel)

Bossy Billionaire (A Hero Club Novel)

Love Shorts-A Collection of Short Stories

Thank you so much for reading, and if you enjoyed the crazy ride and decide to leave a review, we'd truly appreciate the support.

About the Author

Chiquita Dennie is an author of Contemporary, Romantic Suspense, Erotic, Thriller, Mystery, and Women's Fiction. Chiquita lives in Los Angeles, CA. Before she started writing contemporary romance, she worked in the entertainment industry on notable TV shows such as *The Dr Phil Show*, *The Tyra Banks Show*, *American Idol*, and *Deal or No Deal*. But her favorite job is the one she's now doing full time: writing romance.

A best-selling author and award-winning filmmaker, her first short film *Invisible* was released in summer 2017 and screened in multiple festivals and won for Best Short Film. Also, she hosts a podcast that showcases the latest in beauty, business, and community called "Moscato and Tea." Her debut release of Antonio and Sabrina *Struck In Love* has opened a new avenue of writing that she loves.

If you want to know when the next book will come out, please visit her website at http://www.chiquitadennie.com, where you can sign up to receive an email for her next release.

304 Publishing Company

We showcase books about African American, Interracial, Women's Fiction, Erotic, and Contemporary Romance novels. Along with Thriller, Suspense, Poetry, Beauty, and Style Books. Thank you for taking the time out to visit. Join our mailing list to stay updated with new releases and blog posts.

www.ingramcontent.com/pod-product-compliance
Lightning Source LLC
Chambersburg PA
CBHW011200190726
48286CB00009B/2859